On the Bus, On the Case

by Steve Brezenoff   Illustrated by C.B. Canga

r Samantha Archer,

Field Trip Mysteries are published by Stone Arch Books
A Capstone Imprint
1710 Roe Crest Drive
North Mankato, Minnesota 56003
www.capstonepub.com

Library of Congress Cataloging-in-Publication Data is
available on the Library of Congress website.

ISBN: 978-1-4342-2531-3

Graphic Designers:
Kay Fraser
Carla Zetina-Yglesias

Printed in the United States of America
in Stevens Point, Wisconsin.
022014   008033

★ THE FIELD TRIPS ★

FRANKLIN MIDDLE SCHOOL

SCIENTIA EST POTENTIA

EST. 1889

Dear parent/guardian of James Shoo,

Ms. Stanwyck's art class is going on a field trip!

We will be traveling to the River City Art Museum as part of our unit on painting.

We have been promised that no one will be stealing priceless art from the museum while our class is visiting.

Please sign and return this form as soon as possible so that your child will be allowed to attend the field trip.

Cindy Shoo

Parent/Guardian Signature

The Painting That Wasn't There

James Shoo

A.K.A: Gum

D.O.B: November 19th

POSITION: 6th Grade

Is this because he chews a lot of gum?

INTERESTS:

Gum-chewing, field trips, and showing everyone what a crook Anton Gutman is.

KNOWN ASSOCIATES:

Archer, Samantha; Duran, Catalina; and Garrison, Edward.

NOTES:

Mr. Spade has made an effort to stop James from chewing gum in class. We fear he cannot be stopped.

★ TABLE OF CONTENTS ★

CHAPTER ONE

GUM SHOO

My name is James Shoo.

No one calls me that, though.

Everyone calls me Gum instead.

Kids who don't know me too well think that's because I always chew gum, but they're wrong.

I mean, I do always chew gum. Gum is probably my favorite thing in the world.

I love almost every flavor I've ever tried: watermelon, green apple, cotton candy . . . you name it. So I do chew gum pretty much nonstop when I'm awake.

My mom makes me eat other foods too, of course. It's hard to eat food of any kind while chewing gum. But once I finish eating, it's right back to the gum.

Still, that's not why I'm called Gum.

Anton Gutman, this total dork in our class, says it's because "gum" rhymes with "dumb." That's one of many reasons my friends and I don't like Anton Gutman.

My best friends know the real reason I'm called Gum. Actually, my friend Sam — Samantha Archer, that is — gave me the name.

Sam lives with her grandparents, and she watches old detective movies with them all the time. So she's always using funny words and phrases normal people haven't said in, like, a hundred years.

"Gumshoe" is one of those words, I guess.

Anyway, she started calling me Gum Shoo after our first adventure. That's what this story is about.

It all started in Ms. Stanwyck's art class.

MY FRIENDS

Every Monday afternoon, my sixth-grade class has art class. We get to leave our normal classroom and go down to the art room.

I love Monday afternoons.

Pretty much everyone does. It's fun to leave Mr. Spade's class and go to Ms. Stanwyck's art class.

Her classroom is colorfully decorated, with paintings and photographs. It's different from our normal classroom.

I like Ms. Stanwyck because she never gives me a hard time about chewing gum in class.

My friend Egg loves art class more than most of us. He's really into photography, and some weeks, we take pictures.

"I really hope that Ms. Stanwyck is going to have us do photography today," Egg whispered to me as we headed down the hall.

Egg wasn't named for his favorite breakfast. His real name is Edward G. Garrison: E.G.G. So everyone just calls him Egg. Besides loving photography, he's also pretty much the shortest kid in our grade.

We were following single-file behind Mr. Spade, our teacher. Egg was walking right behind me. In front of me was our friend Cat, and in front of Cat was Sam.

Sam is the tallest kid in our grade. She's taller than Mr. Spade, even.

"You always say that!" Sam said to Egg. "We can't do photography in art class every week!"

Egg shrugged. "I don't see why not," he said. He raised his camera and snapped a photo of Sam.

That camera was always around Egg's neck. It's digital, but it's huge. It looks funny on such a little guy. It's almost bigger than he is.

Right before we reached Ms. Stanwyck's class, I reached into my pocket and pulled out a fresh piece of gum.

Orange-flavored gum, to be exact.

The gum in my mouth was losing its flavor: root beer float.

"Ms. Stanwyck told us last week that we'd be looking at paintings," Cat reminded us. "Sorry, Egg, no photography today."

"Oh well," Egg said. "Maybe next time. I guess paintings could be cool too."

We didn't realize it then, but our adventure was about to begin.

CHAPTER THREE

ART CLASS

When everybody reached the art room and sat down, Ms. Stanwyck gave us all a **big smile.**

She's a very nice lady. She's about as old as the hills, and she's even shorter than Egg. She always has a pair of old glasses hanging around her neck.

"Let's start by looking at a couple of paintings," our teacher said.

Ms. Stanwyck switched off the lights and switched on the projector.

"Each of the paintings I'm going to show you is considered a masterpiece," she said. "They have something else in common, though."

The first painting was of a man and his dog. The man was carrying a basket under one arm. The painting looked very old.

"This one is called *After the Hunt*," Ms. Stanwyck said. "It's by Jan Weenix. He painted it in 1665."

"Aw, cute, a doggy!" Cat called out.

Some kids laughed. Cat sat back and smiled. She loves animals.

"Wait, what's in the basket?" Sam added, leaning forward.

"Whoa, it's a bunch of dead birds," I pointed out.

Cat's jaw dropped. "And is he also carrying a dead bunny?" she asked.

"That's right," Ms. Stanwyck replied. "Remember, it's called *After the Hunt*."

"I don't like it," Cat whispered.

Ms. Stanwyck clicked her controller and the next slide came up. This one looked like the inside of a barn. There were some people and horses.

"Ooh, horses!" Cat exclaimed.

"This painting is my favorite," Ms. Stanwyck said. "It is by a man named George Morland. It's called *The Inside of a Stable*, from 1791. It's considered Morland's finest work. Many young artists have made copies of it as they learned how to paint."

Ms. Stanwyck stopped and looked around the class. "Have any of you figured out what these paintings have in common?" she asked us.

Sam raised her hand. "Is it that they have animals in them?" she asked.

Ms. Stanwyck nodded. "That's right, Samantha," she said. "Even more exciting, though, is that all the paintings I'm showing you today are on tour."

"On tour?" I said, laughing. "Like a band? I can't really see these paintings selling out the arena!"

"Well, something like that," Ms. Stanwyck said, smiling. "Sometimes very famous paintings are sent from city to city so people all over the world can see them in person."

"All these paintings are coming to River City?" Cat asked. She sounded excited. "A tour of animal paintings! I can't wait!"

"You won't have to wait long," Ms. Stanwyck said. "We'll be going on a field trip to the Art Museum next Monday."

"Yes!" I said, pumping my fist. "I love a good field trip."

"I'm glad you're all so excited," Ms. Stanwyck said. "I'm excited myself. *The Inside of a Stable* is the featured painting. I haven't seen it since I made my own copy of it back in art school."

I frowned. This didn't make any sense to me at all. Why would she make a copy of a painting?

"Ms. Stanwyck, I don't get it," I said. "Can't you just scan it, or take a picture or something? Seems like a big pain to copy it!"

Ms. Stanwyck smiled at me. "Well, James," she said, "we don't make copies just to have a copy. Young artists make copies to learn techniques, or to challenge themselves."

"Why do so many people copy this painting?" Cat said. "Is it because they think the small horse is cute?"

Ms. Stanwyck looked lovingly at the slide. Then she looked back at us.

"Not exactly. You see, students, George Morland's style is very casual," she said. "He never put a lot of work into his paintings. They were quickly done, and sometimes sloppy."

"So they're easier to copy?" asked Sam.

"Well, you'd think so . . . at first," Ms. Stanwyck said. She smiled again.

"Many art students try to copy Morland's strokes exactly," she told us. "That's very difficult to do. If you look closely, you can see where Morland did a stroke quickly."

Ms. Stanwyck pointed to the small wheelbarrow in the corner of the painting. "This part was difficult for me," she said. "But you can see what a quick job Morland made of it. It's very sloppy!"

She added, "Come and have a closer look if you like. Then we'll move on to some more paintings."

Sam, Egg, Cat, and I gathered around the painting.

Some other kids in the class got up to look closer too.

Egg took a quick photo of the wheelbarrow.

"You can see how the brush left a mark here," he said, pointing. "Cool!"

We had a look and then went to sit down. Then Ms. Stanwyck went on to show us about a million more paintings, but the real excitement started a week later.

CHAPTER FOUR

THE MUSEUM

The next Monday, instead of going to Ms. Stanwyck's classroom for art, we all boarded a school bus for our field trip. Egg and I shared the last seat of the bus, and Sam and Cat sat across the aisle from us.

The road from the school to the Art Museum was very bumpy. Every bump we hit sent the four of us flying straight up. Sam almost banged her head on the bus ceiling like ten times. It was fun.

We hit another bump and Egg went flying. "Woo!" he cried out. He was the smallest, so he always got the most air. The camera around his neck almost fell off.

"Are you going to take photos of the paintings, Egg?" Cat asked. "And can I have copies?"

"Sure," Egg replied.

Ms. Stanwyck called back to us, "Remember, Edward: you can take photos, but don't use the flash."

Egg nodded. "I know," he said. "Because the flash can damage the paintings."

"That's right," Ms. Stanwyck said. "It can fade the colors."

Soon the bus pulled up to the curb in front of the museum. We all piled out onto the sidewalk. It was a very sunny morning.

We all gathered around Ms. Stanwyck and rushed into the museum. The entrance was amazing! It was this huge room, with a big domed ceiling. It looked like everything was made of marble and gold.

A few men and women in blue suits stood around. They all had badges on their jackets. One of them looked at us and said, "Shhh!"

"Sure is a lot of muscle in here," Sam muttered to us, frowning at the security guards.

Cat and Egg looked at me. "Huh?" they both said.

I whispered to my friends, "Sam means there are a lot of security guards. I think."

Sometimes we need to help each other understand Sam when she uses expressions from those old movies she loves.

Cat nodded. "Got it," she whispered back. Then the four of us followed the rest of the class.

Ms. Stanwyck led us down a long hallway. The walls were lined with loads of paintings, but none of them had any animals in them.

"Ms. Stanwyck," Cat called out, "wait just a second. There are no animals in these paintings!"

Ms. Stanwyck laughed. "Don't worry, Catalina," she said. "The exhibit we're here to see has a room all to itself, at the end of this hall."

Soon we came to an archway. We went through it into a huge circular room.

I gasped. The room looked bigger than a football field!

The walls were covered with paintings. A circle of metal posts and a velvet rope made it impossible to get very close to the paintings.

"Wow," Egg whispered. Even though he was trying to be quiet, his voice bounced off the walls.

We walked lightly after Ms. Stanwyck, and our steps echoed and squeaked on the stone floor.

Ms. Stanwyck stopped right in the middle of the room. We all gathered around her.

"Okay, students," she said. "I want you to walk around and look at the paintings, and talk to each other about the paintings. In class next week, we'll discuss what we've seen here."

She looked at her watch. "The time is now eight o'clock. We will have three hours in the museum. Meet back here at eleven o'clock sharp. No excuses for being late!"

"Yes, Ms. Stanwyck," the whole class said together.

Our group of four stuck together, as usual. That's what best friends do, even on field trips.

"Look at this one," Cat cried out. She grabbed Sam and pulled her toward a painting.

Egg and I followed them.

Cat had taken us to a painting of two horses, one black and one white.

A man in blue was sitting on the black one. Both horses were having a drink from a small pond.

"I like the white horse," Cat said. "This is an awesome painting."

Sam shrugged. "It's okay, I guess," she said. "It's nothing special, though. Just a couple of old horses."

Egg scratched his chin. "I wonder why that guy has two horses," he said.

His glasses slid down his nose, and he carefully pushed them back up.

I leaned on Egg's shoulder. "Who knows!" I said. "Maybe he was out riding the black horse and this white horse just started following him."

"Right," Sam said, laughing. "So the guy in blue thinks, 'Hey, free horse! I'm going to keep him.'"

"That's probably what I'd think," I replied.

"Me too," Egg said. "I like it. I think I'm going to take pictures of all of our favorites."

We all made room so that he could take a good photo.

Then Egg snapped a few pictures of other paintings, too.

"Hey!" someone shouted.

The four of us spun around.

It was the security guard who had shushed us earlier.

"No flash photography!" he said.

The security guard walked over to us and grabbed Egg's collar and his camera.

Egg cowered. "The f-flash didn't go off," he said, stuttering a little.

Egg gets nervous sometimes. "I know that's bad for the paintings," he added. "I w-wouldn't use a flash around them. I swear."

Egg was right, I'm sure of it. There was no flash when he took the picture. So I said so. "He's right, mister. The flash didn't go off."

Sam and Cat nodded. "He knows a lot about photography," Cat added.

The guard glared at us. "This is your first and only warning," he said. Then he handed Egg his camera, let go of his collar, and walked off.

THE SUSPECTS

The four of us huddled together. "What was that all about?" Cat asked in a whisper.

Sam squinted at the security guard, whose back was to us. "I don't know," she said. "But he's cruising for a bruising."

Sam was talking like an old-time detective again.

"Is he?" Egg asked.

Sam nodded. "Yep," she said. "If he keeps giving you a hard time, Egg, he's in trouble with me."

Suddenly, Cat clapped her hands together. "Look!" she said. "It's the painting Ms. Stanwyck loved so much."

We all turned and looked where Cat was looking.

She was right. It was the painting Ms. Stanwyck had copied in art school: *The Inside of a Stable*, by George Morland.

Most of our classmates were already surrounding the painting. Of course, no one could get too close, because of the velvet rope.

Even the security guard had gone over there. I guess that was because the crowd was so big.

The group of us had made him pretty nervous, too. He was all shaky and sweating. Most days he doesn't usually have to watch so many people at once!

We walked over to the group.

"I can't get very close," Cat said sadly.

"Wait a few minutes," I replied. "People will move on to other paintings pretty soon."

"I don't need to wait," Egg said. "I can sneak through the crowd and snap a quick shot."

He started to weave through the group of students.

"Watch yourself, Egg," Sam called after him. "That goon has his eye on you."

Egg turned around and looked at me.

"She means the security guard," I said. "No flash photos."

Egg nodded. "I know," he said. "Don't worry." With that, he slid into the crowd and vanished.

A moment later, the security guard screamed, "Hey! I said no flash photography!"

He dove into the crowd of students. Soon he had Egg by the collar in one hand, and Egg's camera in the other hand.

"My flash didn't go off," Egg shouted in reply.

The guard put Egg down at the back of the crowd, next to Ms. Stanwyck.

"I promise, Ms. Stanwyck," Egg pleaded. "My flash didn't go off!"

"I'm sorry," the guard said, "but I'm going to have to confiscate this camera until your group leaves the museum at eleven."

"No," Egg said. "I need my camera. I have to have my camera. That is totally unfair. Please, I swear, I didn't use a flash, and I need to have my camera!"

Ms. Stanwyck looked at the guard, then at Egg. "Edward," she said, "the guard has to have the final say in this matter."

"But, Ms. Stanwyck . . . ," Egg started to say, but Ms. Stanwyck stopped him by putting up her hand.

"Now, Edward," she said, frowning at him, "it's really not like you to talk back. You will have your camera back in a few hours."

"Yes, Ms. Stanwyck," Egg said, looking at his feet.

"Good," Ms. Stanwyck said. "Now go enjoy the museum with your friends."

Egg walked over to me, Sam, and Cat. "I can't believe this!" he shouted. "This is so unfair."

Sam put a hand on his shoulder. "It's okay, Egg," she said. "That stooge had it in for you, but you'll get your camera back."

"Oh, I know that," Egg said. "There's something else. The painting by Morland. I got a good look at it with my telephoto lens."

"And?" Cat prompted.

Egg took a deep breath and pushed his glasses up his nose. "It's a copy," he said. "A fake!"

CHAPTER SIX

ART SCHOOL

"A fake?" I said, shocked. "How can you tell?"

"I got a very good look at the bottom right corner," Egg said. "I wanted to see the wheelbarrow."

"The part Ms. Stanwyck said was hard to copy?" Cat asked.

Egg nodded. "Right," he said. "Well, in the painting up there, you can tell it's not his sloppy, quick strokes. You can tell the person who painted that painting was being really, really careful."

"Like someone was trying too hard?" Sam asked.

Egg nodded again. "Exactly," he said. "Not like someone was being fast. Like they were being slow and taking their time."

"Why would the museum hang up a fake painting?" I asked.

Not that I didn't trust Egg. It was just that it didn't make sense. Why would a museum have a fake in its collection? I didn't get it.

"I get it," Sam said.

"You do?" I asked, feeling confused.

Sam nodded slowly. "I can see it now," she said.

"Well, you're going to have to explain it to me," I told her. "Because I don't get it and I can't see it."

Sam smiled. "With all this muscle around, these paintings must be worth a pretty penny," she began.

"Obviously," I said. "They hired a lot of security to protect the paintings."

"Right," Sam said. She thought for a second. "So if someone made a copy of one of the paintings," she went on, "that person could switch it with the real painting on the wall. Then the crook would have the real painting, which is worth a fortune! Maybe millions!"

"Whoa," Egg said. "Millions?"

Sam shrugged. "Could be. I've heard of paintings selling for hundreds of millions of dollars."

"Wait a second. If that's a copy of the Morland horse painting," Cat said, frowning, "shouldn't we tell Ms. Stanwyck?"

"Or the police?" I added.

Sam shook her head. "There's no good proof," she said.

"Right," Egg added, nodding. "The security guard took my camera. The photo I took of the wheelbarrow is still in it."

"So?" I said. "The painting itself is right there on the wall. Anyone can just walk up to it and check it out!"

"Not really," Cat said. "The velvet rope makes it impossible to get close."

We all fell silent and thought about it.

Sam finally spoke. "You know what we have to do," she said. "Solve this crime ourselves."

She and I looked at each other and nodded. "Okay," I said.

Egg nodded and said, "I'm in. Definitely."

Cat sighed. "You guys," she said. "Fine. Me too."

Sam beamed. "All right," she said. "A real mystery. First, we need a list of suspects!"

"Anton Gutman," I said right away. "He's the suspect at the top of the list."

"Anton?" Cat asked. "What does he have to do with it?"

I shrugged. "Whatever," I said. "I don't like him!"

"Fine," Sam said. "So Anton is on our suspect list. But who else?"

"Isn't it obvious, you guys?" Cat whispered. "It was Ms. Stanwyck!"

I nearly fell over. "Ms. Stanwyck?" I said. "Are you crazy? Why would she steal the painting?"

Sam stroked her chin. "Maybe Cat has a point," she said. "We already know she made a copy of the painting in question. She admitted that much in class last week, remember?"

"That's true," I said, nodding.

"Plus," Sam put in, "she knows everything about Morland and this painting. Even from ten feet away, she must have been able to spot a fake. Why didn't she say anything?"

"Hm," Egg added. "She did let that security guard take my camera, too."

"The only evidence," Sam pointed out.

"Okay then," I said. "Fine. I'll add Ms. Stanwyck to the suspect list."

Just then, the security guard came over.

"What are you kids up to over here?" the guard asked.

"Nothing, sir," Cat replied with a big smile.

The guard eyed Egg. "Make sure it stays that way," the guard said. He glared at each of us, then walked off.

As the security guard walked away, a weird guy in a long coat knocked into him.

"Excuse me," the weird guy said.

Something fell out of the guard's back pocket.

"What's that?" I said, pointing.

Cat jogged over and scooped it up. "Sir!" she started to call out. But then she suddenly stopped.

Cat came darting back over to us. "Guys," she said. "Check this out." She held out a folded piece of thick paper.

"A brochure?" Egg said.

Sam grabbed it and looked at the cover. "Not just any brochure," she said. "It's a brochure for an art school!"

"The guard is an art student too?" I said.

"Plus he has access to the museum and all the paintings," Cat added.

"You know what that means," Egg said.

Sam nodded and whispered, "It means our suspect list just got one name longer."

AHA!

"So," I said, popping a fresh piece of strawberry-banana gum into my mouth, "our suspects so far are Ms. Stanwyck, the security guard who took Egg's camera, and . . ."

Just then, someone bumped into me.

Anton Gutman.

"Oh, sorry," Anton said, laughing.

He and two of his weaselly friends were walking past us, giggling and hiding something.

"What are those clowns up to?" Sam asked.

I shrugged. "No good, I bet," I said.

We watched as Anton and his friends went into the nearest restroom.

"Let's follow them," Sam said.

"Gross!" Cat replied quickly.

Sam rolled her eyes. "We have to see what they're hiding," she said.

"We'll go," I said, taking Egg by the arm.

"Wait a second. What? We will?" Egg protested. But I pulled him along next to me.

Quietly, I pushed the bathroom door open. Anton and his friends were standing, thick as thieves, at the sinks. They were still giggling. They didn't hear us come in.

"Aha!" I shouted, pointing at them. "Caught you!"

The three hoodlums jumped. But they weren't huddling around any stolen painting. They were busy writing their names on the bathroom mirror.

"What do you think you're doing?" I said when I saw the permanent markers in their hands.

They glanced over at me and Egg. I guess they figured we couldn't stop them.

Anton just laughed and turned back to the mirror. "Go away, losers," he said.

I was ready to get out of there. Anton wasn't the crook. I thought Egg was turning to leave. But instead, he turned and opened the bathroom door. Then he shouted out into the hallway, "Guard!"

"Hey!" Anton yelled. "Shut up, Egg!"

But it was too late. The security guard came running.

Egg and I got out of the way. We watched the guard drag away Anton's gang by their collars. I have to say, it felt good to see justice being served.

We walked back over to Cat and Sam and told them what had happened.

"Well, I guess Anton isn't a suspect anymore," I said.

"Yeah," Egg agreed. "He's still a jerk, though."

"I can't believe you called the guard," Cat said.

Egg laughed. "Me either. But those guys totally deserve it."

"Totally," Cat said. "I mean, are we in third grade anymore? Who writes their name in the bathroom? How stupid."

"Back to the mystery, guys. So if Anton isn't a suspect, that leaves Ms. Stanwyck and the guard," Sam said, counting on her fingers.

Just then, I spotted that weird guy in the long coat and old-fashioned hat again. This time he was skulking around near the Morland painting.

I elbowed Sam.

When she looked over at me, I whispered, "Hey, look at that guy." I pointed at the man and added, "Doesn't he look shady?"

Sam nodded slowly. "Definitely," she replied. "Why do you think he's hanging around by the Morland painting?"

"Pretty suspicious," Egg agreed.

Cat nodded. The four of us moved in to check out the weird guy.

"Over here," Sam said.

We followed her into a doorway near the Morland painting and huddled together.

"He's hiding something under that coat, I bet," Sam said.

"Yeah," Cat agreed. "It's too hot out for a coat like that."

"Exactly," Sam said. "In the old movies crooks wears coats like that all the time. He's involved with this crime. I just know it."

"I'm with Sam," I said, nodding. "He looks like a crook."

Suddenly, a voice came from behind us. "All right, Mel," the voice said. "My shift is over. I'll see you tomorrow."

It was the security guard who'd taken Egg's camera. The doorway we had hidden in was the entrance to the security guards' break room.

We turned to look. The guard was picking up a long black case.

"What have you got there, Tom?" the other guard said.

That must have been Mel. Tom was the security guard who had taken Egg's camera, of course.

Tom looked at the case in his hand. "What, this?" he said. "Oh, it's just my pool cue."

"Off to shoot some pool this afternoon?" Mel asked.

"That's right," Tom replied. "Well, I'll see ya tomorrow."

With that, the guard started walking toward us. He stopped when he reached the doorway where we were.

"You kids sneaking around again?" he asked.

"Don't worry. Mel in there will give your camera back when your group is ready to leave."

The man shook his head and started walking off.

"Speaking of that," I said, "what time is it, Egg?"

Egg looked at his wrist. "It's ten-thirty," he replied.

"Ten-thirty?!" Sam said. "That only gives us thirty minutes to crack this case!"

CASE CRACKED!

"Okay," I said. "Let's think."

Cat nodded and said, "Right. What do we know?"

Sam took a deep breath. "We know that Ms. Stanwyck knows everything about Morland," she said. "And we know she made a copy of *The Inside of a Stable*."

"We know the guard is in art school," Egg added, "or thinking about going to art school."

"Right," Cat said. "So he may have made a copy of the Morland painting too."

"And," Sam added, "we spotted that shady guy skulking near the painting."

I shook my head. "This is getting us nowhere," I said. "We must be missing something."

The four of us leaned against the cold marble wall. I was feeling pretty down about this mystery.

From where I was standing, I could see a cleaning crew. A couple of men in green uniforms were taking down a painting. First they pulled the painting off the wall. Then one man pulled the frame off.

Without the frame, the painting was just a big piece of canvas.

The second man picked up the canvas and rolled it up, like a poster. Then he slid it into a long case with a zipper at the top.

"That's it!" I shouted, jumping to my feet.

"What's it?" Sam said.

"No time to explain," I replied. "Just follow me. We have to run!"

I started down the hall toward the main entrance.

My sneakers squeaked on the hard floor. The sound echoed through the museum.

My three best friends were close at my heels.

"Where are we going?" Sam said as she caught up to me. Sam is very fast.

"We have to catch that security guard before he leaves," I replied between breaths.

I looked around. The guard was slowly walking toward the exit. "See you tomorrow, guys," he said, waving at the other guards. They all smiled at him and waved.

"Stop him!" I shouted before he could leave. "He stole a painting!"

The guards turned and looked at me. They all looked really confused. I could feel my face turning red.

"What are you talking about, kid?" one of the other guards said.

"He stole that Morland painting," I said, standing firm.

"What?" another guard said. "No way. The Morland painting is still hanging in the gallery."

"That's a copy," Egg said.

"Ask him what's in that black case," I said. "That will prove it."

Tom laughed. "This?" he said. "This is my pool cue." He turned to the other guards. "You guys know how much I love to shoot pool!" he said.

The other guards nodded. "Tom shoots pool a few times a week," one of them said. "I've seen his cue case lots of times."

Tom shook his head. Once again, he started for the door.

Just then, the weird man in the overcoat stepped up and took Tom's arm. "Just a moment please," the weird guy said. "I think maybe we should have a look in that case."

"Hey!" Tom replied. "Who do you think you are?"

The weird guy pulled a leather case from his coat pocket. He flipped it open to reveal a gold badge. "I'm Detective Jones, River City Police Department," he said. "Open the case."

"I knew that guy was involved somehow," Sam whispered.

"I won't!" Tom said. "I know my rights."

The detective nodded. "Very well," he said. "Let's all go take a closer look at the painting on the wall."

Tom swallowed. "O-okay," he said.

The detective led us and Tom back to the exhibit. He found Ms. Stanwyck and asked her to step past the velvet rope.

"Get a close look, Ms. Stanwyck," the detective said.

"At the wheelbarrow!" Egg added.

Ms. Stanwyck looked at the detective and Egg. "Okay," she said. She pulled a magnifying glass from her pocket.

"That explains why she didn't spot it earlier," Sam whispered. "Her vision isn't good enough."

"They're right!" Ms. Stanwyck suddenly exclaimed. "These strokes are definitely not Morland's! This copy isn't even as good as the one I made years ago."

The detective glared at Tom the security guard. "You ready to open that case now?" Detective Jones asked.

Tom unzipped the top of the case and pulled out a pool cue. "See?" he said. "Just a pool cue!"

"Just a pool cue, huh?" I said.

Then I suddenly snatched at the case. I reached in and pulled out a rolled-up canvas.

"What's this?" I said. I unrolled the canvas, showing the real *The Inside of a Stable*.

The detective smiled at us. "Nice job, kids," he said.

"He figured it out," Sam said, pointing at me.

"What's your name, kid?" Detective Jones asked.

"Shoo," I replied. "James Shoo."

"You're a real detective, James Shoo," Detective Jones said, patting my shoulder.

"You could say," Sam added with a chuckle, "he's a real gumshoe."

Cat, Egg, and I all looked at her.

"Get it?" Sam said. "Gumshoe?"

We all shook our heads.

Sam sighed. "It's old-movie slang for detective," she said. "And James's name is Shoo?!"

I rolled my eyes and we all made fun of Sam, but really I liked the nickname.

So it stuck, and that's why I'm called Gum Shoo.

THE
END

FRANKLIN MIDDLE SCHOOL
SCIENTIA EST POTENTIA
EST. 1889

Dear parent/guardian of Samantha Archer,

The sixth grade is going on a field trip!

We will be traveling to Scrub Brush for the weekend.
We'll learn about how Americans lived during
frontier times.

*Don't worry. No one will be trying to close down the town while
we are there.*

Please sign and return this form as soon as possible so
that your child will be allowed to attend the field trip.

Ruth Archer
Parent/Guardian Signature

THE VILLAGE THAT ALMOST VANISHED

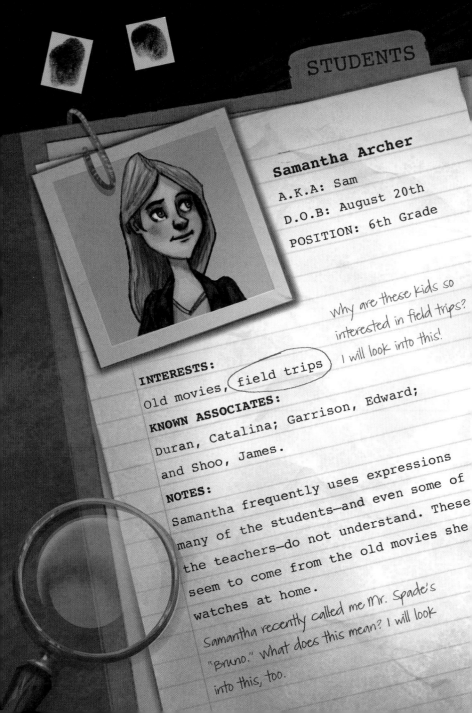

Samantha Archer

A.K.A: Sam

D.O.B: August 20th

POSITION: 6th Grade

Why are these kids so interested in field trips? I will look into this!

INTERESTS:

Old movies, (field trips)

KNOWN ASSOCIATES:

Duran, Catalina; Garrison, Edward; and Shoo, James.

NOTES:

Samantha frequently uses expressions many of the students—and even some of the teachers—do not understand. These seem to come from the old movies she watches at home.

Samantha recently called me Mr. Spade's *"Bruno." What does this mean? I will look into this, too.*

★ TABLE OF CONTENTS ★

ONE HOT FRIDAY

I'm Samantha Archer.
You can call me Sam.

I'm twelve years old,
five feet and eight inches tall,
and I solve crimes with
some help from my friends.

My friends and I have caught lots of crooks, usually when we go on field trips together. We all have our favorite tales about the cases we've solved, and this is mine.

It all started on a hot Friday morning. Egg and I were sitting on the curb in front of our school. He was fiddling with his camera, like always. If you want to solve crimes, get a friend with a camera. Those pictures are great evidence.

Egg's duffel bag was next to him on the curb. We were both packed for a weekend away from home.

We were going on a field trip!

We go on lots of field trips at our school. They're usually pretty fun, and they're almost always exciting. But this field trip was the biggest of the year. Maybe the biggest of our whole lives.

This was the annual sixth-grade weekend trip to Scrub Brush. That's an old ghost town in the middle of nowhere.

Fifty years ago, some rich guy bought the whole empty town. He decided to turn the place into a living history lesson. He brought in actors to play cowboys and saloon keepers and gold prospectors.

Now, schools visited all the time. Sixth graders from Franklin Middle School got to go every year. We'd been looking forward to this trip for a long time.

We were really excited.

"Boy, it's hot today," Egg said.

"Yep," I said.

Just then, a shadow fell over me. I looked up and saw Anton Gutman.

"Hello, dorks," Anton said.

"Hello, Gutman," I replied. "Shouldn't you be getting into trouble someplace else?"

"Oh, I'll be getting into trouble," Anton said. He held up his overnight bag. "I have more tricks and practical jokes in this bag than you can imagine," he said with a chuckle.

"Mr. Spade will catch you," Egg said.

"Nah," Anton replied.

I shrugged. "Then we will," I said.

"Ooh, I'm so scared," Anton said. Then he walked away.

I looked down the street. "Here come Gum and Cat," I said.

Our friends were strolling like turtles down the sidewalk toward us. I couldn't blame them. Moving fast only made it feel hotter.

Finally they reached us. The four of us walked over to the bus.

The whole sixth grade was standing around our teacher, Mr. Spade. He looked at his watch. "Well, that's everyone," he said. "Let's go."

He got on the bus. All the kids piled on after him. The four of us sat in the back.

We were off on the most exciting field trip of our lives! Of course, we had no idea just how exciting it would be.

CHAPTER TWO

THE LONG ROAD

It's a long ride to Scrub Brush.

After an hour or so, the bus pulled off the road.

"Are we there?" Egg said.

"Can't be," I said. "We're only an hour from school. Scrub Brush is way farther than that."

Mr. Spade got up from his seat and faced the students. "Okay, everyone," he said. "We're going to take a break now."

I looked out the window. We were in front of a big gas station with a fast food place attached to it. A big sign read "BIG Stop." BIG Stop is a really popular fast food chain where we live. There are dozens of them.

"We'll get moving again in about twenty minutes," Mr. Spade said.

Cat and I went into the little restaurant. "I want to grab some fries," I said.

I ran to the counter and nearly knocked down an old man in a cowboy hat. He had been talking to a young woman in a business suit.

"Sorry," I said.

The man went back to talking to the young woman. I ordered some fries.

"I don't care what your offer is," the old man said. "I'm not selling my land to BIG Stop."

The woman sighed. She seemed upset. "If you change your mind, you know how to find me," she said. "Mr. G. won't be happy about this."

The old man didn't say anything. He just turned and walked off.

I watched the woman. Suddenly she faced me.

"What do you want?" she snapped.

I must have jumped about thirty feet. "Um, nothing," I stammered.

I forgot about my fries and headed for the door. Cat was waiting for me with Egg and Gum.

Mr. Spade was standing by the door of the bus as we got back on.

"Everyone, take a ticket from me as you get back on the bus please," Mr. Spade said.

He handed me a big blue ticket. "What's this for?" I asked.

"That's your ticket to Scrub Brush," Mr. Spade said. "You need that to get in."

"How much longer is the drive?" Gum asked as he took his own ticket.

"About another hour," Mr. Spade replied.

Once everyone was on the bus, we got settled in for some more driving.

I stared out the window. My stomach was rumbling. I wished I hadn't forgotten about my fries.

TWO RIDERS

We'd been on the road for another hour
when the brakes squealed and the bus
stopped.

Mr. Spade got up from his seat. The
driver shut off the bus and pulled open the
door.

"Okay, everyone," Mr. Spade said.
"We're here! Grab your bags!"

Gum stepped off the bus right before I
did. "Whoa," he said.

As my foot hit the dry ground, I looked
up the road.

Through the reddish dust, I could see several old, small buildings. It seemed like no one had been there for a hundred years.

Mr. Spade scratched his head. "Hmm," he mumbled. "I thought someone would be here to meet us."

Suddenly we heard a quiet clomp, clomp.

I shielded my eyes and gazed up the road. Through the dust, I spotted two figures moving toward us.

"Look, over there!" I said, pointing. "I see two people riding horses, and they're coming this way!"

Egg tried to take a photo, but it was too dusty to get a good shot. "Darn," he said, rubbing his camera's lens with the bottom of his shirt. "I hope this isn't a problem all weekend!"

The riders were getting closer.

"Welcome to Scrub Brush, kids," one of them called.

The two riders reached us. One was a man with a huge mustache and dark hair. The other was a young woman. Both had shiny star-shaped badges on their shirts, and they were both wearing cowboy hats. They got off their horses.

"I'm Sheriff Bob Grady. You can call me Sheriff Bob," the man said.

The woman pulled off her hat. "And I'm Deputy Laura Curtin," she said. "You can call me Deputy Laurie."

"It's great to meet you," Mr. Spade said, shaking their hands. "You weren't here last year, were you?"

Mr. Spade had been the sixth-grade teacher for years. He would have known the sheriff and deputy if they'd been there before.

"Nope," Sheriff Bob said. "We both joined Scrub Brush's law enforcement this season. Deputy Laurie will collect your tickets. I need to get back to town."

The sheriff put one foot in his horse's stirrup and swung up onto the saddle. The horse galloped back to town. The sheriff seemed like he was in a big hurry.

"All right," Deputy Laurie said. "Give me your tickets." She frowned. I wondered if she was angry about something.

Cat and I handed her our tickets. Then we followed Mr. Spade and the rest of the class toward the town. "What's her problem?" Cat whispered.

I shrugged and looked back over my shoulder.

The deputy held the reins of her horse. She started walking slowly back to town.

A THIRD BUNKMATE

"Three beds," Gum said. He sat on one of the tiny beds in the room he was sharing with Egg.

Cat and I had already dropped off our stuff in our room. A third girl, Eliza, was also in our room. She was cool enough.

"I wonder who will be our third person," Egg said, claiming a bed near the window.

Cat sat down. She said, "If there's only one bed left, you will end up with someone who no one else wants to bunk with."

Egg nodded. "Someone who's a big pain," he added.

I sat up straight. "You don't mean . . . ," I said.

"Oh no," Gum added, falling back onto his bed.

CREEEEEAK! The room's door was loud as it swung open.

"Hey, dorks." It was Anton Gutman. He swaggered in and dropped his bag onto the third bed.

"Hi, Anton," Cat said, smiling. She always tries to be pleasant to Anton, even though he calls us dorks.

"You guys are in luck," Anton said. He opened his bag and started digging through it. "You get the famous Anton Gutman in your room with you. Now you're gonna have the best field trip ever."

Gum rolled his eyes. "We need to hurry up," he said. "We're supposed to meet Mr. Spade on Main Street in a few minutes."

"Okay," I said. "Let's get going." I stood up.

Anton waved us off. "I'll meet you there later," he said. "I have some urgent business first."

Anton grabbed his bag of tricks and zipped out the door ahead of us. "What a weirdo," Cat said, shaking her head. "Let's get out of here."

The bunkhouses where we were staying were at the far end of Main Street. Scrub Brush only had two streets, which crossed in the middle of town. One was called Main Street. The other was called First Street. Mr. Spade had asked us to gather at the corner of Main and First after we'd finished getting settled in.

Egg took some pictures as we strolled down Main Street. He took photos of the Saloon, the General Store, the Feed Store, the Jail, and the Sheriff's Office.

As we walked past the Sheriff's Office, we heard some yelling coming from inside.

"What's that shouting?" I asked.

"Sounds like the deputy," Cat said. "And the sheriff."

"They're having an argument," Gum added. "I wonder what they're shouting about."

We all listened, but we couldn't tell what they were saying.

By the time we reached Mr. Spade at the corner, everyone else was already there. Even Anton.

"What took you dorks so long?" Anton asked. Then he started laughing.

The sheriff and deputy walked up. "Okay, everyone," Mr. Spade said. "Sheriff Bob will tell you about today's activities."

"Howdy, kids," Sheriff Bob said. "I'm afraid before we start, I have some bad news."

"You can say that again," Deputy Laurie said under her breath. She looked very angry.

The sheriff glared at her, then went on. "I'm afraid your trip to Scrub Brush might be the last weekend for this camp," he said.

Mr. Spade's eyes shot wide open. "The last weekend?" he asked. "Why?"

"The money from this month's ticket sales has been stolen," the sheriff replied. "If we can't find that money, the land will have to be sold!"

MORE CRIMES

"Can you believe this?" Gum said as the four of us walked down First Street to the first activity.

"I know," Cat said. "We might be the last sixth graders from our school to visit Scrub Brush."

"From any school!" Egg pointed out.

I shrugged. "Of course, we'll have to find the cash," I said.

"Of course," Gum agreed. He blew a big bubble. "But where do we start?"

I thought about it. We didn't have much to go on.

"All we know is that Deputy Laurie and Sheriff Bob had a big fight," I said.

"Don't forget Anton," Gum added.

"You always blame Anton," Egg said. "What makes you think he did it?"

"Are you kidding?" Gum replied. "He's Anton."

I nodded. "True," I said. "Plus, earlier he said he had some urgent business."

Cat nodded. "We'll find more clues," she said. "Don't worry."

We caught up to the rest of the class at the blacksmith. Just as we got there, Mr. Spade and Deputy Laurie were stepping onto the blacksmith shop's porch.

There was a loud crack and then a big boom. The porch collapsed!

"Ah!" Mr. Spade cried out as he fell. The deputy fell right on top of him. They got to their feet quickly.

"What happened?" the sheriff asked as he came running over.

"How should I know?" Deputy Laurie said. "One of the kids could have been hurt!"

Just then, someone poked me in the back. I spun around. I was eye to eye with a short old man. He wore a ragged cowboy hat. He had a funny white mustache and big bushy eyebrows. "That would be a shame, wouldn't it?" the old man said.

"Huh?" I asked. Cat turned around too.

"If one of you kids got hurt," the old man explained. "That would be a shame."

"Sam and Cat," Mr. Spade said. "Please pay attention. We're all going to begin the activity."

We both turned quickly. "Sorry, Mr. Spade," I said. "This old man was —"

But when I turned back, the old man was gone.

I shrugged and looked at Cat. She raised her eyebrows.

The activity was pretty cool. We got to watch the blacksmith make horseshoes and put them on a horse. Then we each got to make our own fire pokers. We all got to swing the blacksmith's hammer. Red sparks flew everywhere!

At the end, we got to keep the fire poker. My grandma would love it. Our fireplace didn't work, but she would love to have the fire poker for a decoration.

After the activity, Mr. Spade led us to the Saloon for lunch. As he opened the swing door, a bucket of red paint came crashing down. Mr. Spade was totally covered in paint.

"What is this?" Mr. Spade cried out. Shocked, he looked down at his shirt and pants.

The sheriff and deputy walked into the Saloon. "What happened?" Sheriff Bob asked.

"What's it look like?" Deputy Laurie said. "Some joke!"

The whole class was totally silent. Except Egg's camera, which was clicking like mad.

"This town sure isn't what it used to be," Mr. Spade muttered. "Falling porches and cans of paint lying around!"

Egg looked around and then whispered to me, "Not to mention the stolen money."

I signaled for Cat and Gum to lean in close.

"Maybe," I said quietly to my friends, "someone really wants to shut down Scrub Brush."

CHAPTER SIX

AROUND THE FIRE

After lunch, we watched Deputy Laurie do a lasso demonstration. Sheriff Bob wasn't around for that.

It was still very hot, but as the day went on, it started to cool down. By supper, it was even getting kind of chilly.

"It can get cold here at night," Mr. Spade said. "We're much higher up than we were back home."

Soon dinner was ready. We all sat at picnic tables to eat our baked beans and hot dogs. (There were even veggie dogs for Cat.)

Each group of bunkmates was supposed to sit together. There were room for two groups at each table. That meant our table was me, Cat, and Eliza, and Gum, Egg, and Anton Gutman.

"This food is gross," Anton said. He crossed his arms when Mr. Spade set a plate in front of him. "I want a BIG Burger with cheese and bacon and hot peppers."

"Well, I guess you're out of luck," Gum replied.

"I also want a BIG Soda," Anton added.

"Anton," I said, "the nearest BIG Stop is over an hour away, remember?"

The sheriff strolled over to us. "You kids enjoying the grub?" he asked. He made a face, like the food didn't look so good to him either.

"It's awful!" Anton replied.

"Don't be rude," Egg said. He took a bite of his hot dog. "It's very good, Sheriff Bob."

The sheriff ignored Egg. "Would you rather have a BIG burger with cheese?" Sheriff Bob asked Anton.

Anton smiled. "Yes, I would!" he replied.

The sheriff leaned down. "To tell you the truth, so would I," he said quietly. "I sure wish there was a BIG Stop near here. I'd take BIG Stop over this place any day!"

Anton nodded. "Me too," he said.

"My mom says BIG Stop food is super unhealthy," Cat said. "I'll stick with these beans."

Just then, Laurie came by. "Leave the kids alone, Bob," she said. Then the sheriff and deputy walked away together, arguing quietly.

"That was weird," I said.

"Yeah," Egg agreed. "Sheriff Bob really loves BIG Stop."

"Hey, Egg," Cat said. "Let's see the pictures you've taken so far."

Anton shook his head. "That sounds boring," he said. Then he got up and walked off.

"Whatever," I said. "Show us those pictures, Egg."

Egg started clicking through the pictures. Soon he came to the ones he had taken at the blacksmith's.

"There's Mr. Spade right before he fell through the porch," Cat pointed out.

"Who's that?" I asked. I pointed to a figure in the background.

"I'm not sure," Gum said. "It kind of looks like Sheriff Bob."

Egg nodded. "The sheriff showed up right after the crash," he said.

"So why is he near the porch before it broke in this picture?" I asked. "That doesn't make sense."

Soon Egg came to the pictures of Mr. Spade covered in red paint.

"Who else was at the Saloon?" I asked.

"I saw Deputy Laurie there," Cat said.

"I didn't see her," I told Cat.

Cat frowned. "I thought it was her. It was someone wearing a big hat. But she just snuck in and then left quickly."

I said, "Maybe she rigged the paint to fall."

"Why would she do that?" Cat asked.

"Who knows?" I said. "Why would Sheriff Bob rig the porch to collapse?"

"Maybe they're working together," Gum suggested.

"Those two?" I said. "No way. They're always fighting."

"Besides, the sheriff is in charge around here," said Egg. "Why would he want to start trouble? It's like, his job to stop trouble!"

"Don't be so sure," said a voice.

I spun around. The creepy old man from the blacksmith's shop was behind me.

"What do you mean?" Gum asked.

"Sheriff Bob Grady doesn't own Scrub Brush," the old man said. He smiled. His teeth were bright white. It looked weird because the rest of him was so dirty and ragged. "But I have a feeling he wants to," the old man added quietly.

I shivered. The old man was seriously creeping me out.

POP! A loud noise came from the campfire. We all turned to look.

"What was that?" Cat asked.

Anton was standing by the fire, laughing.

"Anton!" I said. "He threw a firecracker into the fire."

"He's gone!" Egg said suddenly.

We all turned. The old man had vanished.

DORKS

The next day, we were really up with the roosters. It was early!

Cat and I managed to get dressed and outside fast. Mr. Spade was standing on the walk outside the bunkhouses.

"Good morning, students," he said. "We're going to start today with a visit to the barn. Follow me!"

Soon we got to the barn. Inside, an old woman was sitting on a stool next to a cow. "Gather 'round, y'all," the old woman said. "It's time for me to get the milk you kids will need for your breakfast."

"Gross," Anton Gutman said. "I think I'll have waffles instead of cereal!"

For once I had to agree. I prefer my milk from the fridge, not the cow!

"Daisy Mae is just kidding, kids," Deputy Laurie said. I hadn't even seen her come into the barn. "Don't worry. We buy our milk from the store, just like you do," the deputy added.

That was a relief. We watched Daisy Mae milk the cow. It was weird, but kind of cool.

When she was done, Mr. Spade said, "Time for breakfast. Let's head over to the Saloon."

As we left the barn, Egg grabbed my arm.

"Look," Egg said. "There he is."

Egg pointed to the side of the barn. The old man was there. He looked like he was trying to hide.

"We have to talk to him," I said. "I think he knows something about the weird stuff going on."

"And the stolen money?" Gum asked.

"Maybe," I said. "Come on."

The four of us took off running around the side of the barn. But the old man saw us and ran away.

"Wait!" I called out. "We want to talk to you."

But when we rounded the corner, the old man had vanished completely.

"Boy, he must know this town pretty well," Gum said. "He always just disappears."

"Yeah," Egg agreed, a little out of breath. "And he's in good shape for an old man."

Suddenly we heard yelling. "Samantha Archer!" said Mr. Spade. "Edward! James! Catalina!"

Oops.

Mr. Spade was angry. He came stomping over to us. "What do you think you're doing, running off like that?" he said.

"Sorry, Mr. Spade," I said. I was going to say we were trying to find that old man, but it sounded too weird.

"Ha ha," Anton said from behind Mr. Spade. "What a bunch of dorks."

I don't know about Gum, Cat, and Egg, but I sure felt like a dork right then.

CHAPTER EIGHT

DOWN BY THE RIVER

After breakfast, Deputy Laurie rounded up all us students for the first activity of the day.

"I hear there's a prospector's camp down by the stream," she said. She led us down a dusty path.

We could hear the babbling and bubbling of a small stream. Then, as we came over a rise, we spotted a couple of tents near a brook.

"There they are," the deputy said. **"Let's go check it out."**

We all headed down to the brook. On the shores were three old men. They were using pans and strainers to look for gold in the water.

"Having any luck, boys?" Deputy Laurie asked.

The men didn't say anything, but one of them stood up slowly and turned around. It was the weird old man from town! He winked at me.

"Look!" I said quietly to my friends. "It's him."

Suddenly a loud voice rang out from the town's speaker system: "Deputy Laurie to the office. You have a phone call."

The deputy looked confused. "I'm not expecting any calls," she muttered. "And I can't just leave the class here."

Sheriff Bob walked up. He was holding a leather bag. "You go ahead, Laurie," he said. "I'll stay here with the kids."

Laurie ran off toward the office. "Thanks, Bob," she called back over her shoulder.

The sheriff turned to us. "You kids watch these men work," he said. Then he leaned down and went into one of the prospectors' tents. We all moved closer to the stream.

"What's the pan for?" Gum asked the men. "Are you going to cook some fish?"

One of the old men shook his head. "We're trying to catch something better than fish, son," he said.

"They're looking for gold, Gum," Egg explained.

"That's right," the man said.

"Do you ever find any real gold here?" I asked.

Another man nodded. "With the pans, we scoop up debris from the water," he said. "The strainer holds back anything solid."

"And sometimes," said the first old man, "the solid stuff is gold!"

"Yeehaw!" added the second old man.

"Hey," I said, "where's the third prospector?"

The two men looked at me. "Third prospector?" one asked, frowning. "There's no third man in our camp. Just us two!"

"Oh," I said. "Weird."

We watched them look for gold for a while. After a few moments, the sheriff came out from the tent.

"Okay, kids," he said. "Activity's over. Let's head back."

"We didn't even get to see any gold!" Cat said sadly.

Then I noticed something. "Hey, what happened to the bag you had?" I asked the sheriff.

"What bag?" the sheriff replied.

"You had a leather bag with you when you came down here," Egg said. "I took a photo if you want to see it."

The sheriff laughed. "That's okay, son," he said. Then he added quietly, "That bag wasn't mine. It belonged to one of these men. I was bringing it back for him."

Maybe, I thought, *it was the weird old man's bag. He disappeared right after the sheriff got there!*

THE LAST NIGHT

At the campfire that night, my friends and I sat in a circle.

"If we're going to solve the case of the missing ticket money," Cat said, "we better hurry."

Egg nodded. "Yeah," he said. "We leave in the morning."

"There's Deputy Laurie," I said. "It's time to ask her some questions."

I ran over to the deputy. My friends followed.

"Deputy," I said. "Can I ask you something?"

"Sure," she replied.

"Who called you this morning?" I asked.

The deputy wrinkled her forehead. "That was weird, actually," she replied. "When I got to the office, whoever was on the phone had hung up."

"Hmm," I said. "That is weird."

The deputy walked off.

"Well, that got us nowhere," Egg said.

"Maybe," I replied. "It seems like someone didn't want Deputy Laurie hanging around the prospectors' tents."

I thought for a moment. Then I turned to Egg and said, "Let's take a look at your photos again."

We saw the figure with the big hat again, and the figure with the long hair. One of them showed up in almost every picture, especially when something strange was going on.

"Those two are in all of the pictures," I said.

"Hey, did you guys notice who's missing from all of these pictures?" Gum said.

We thought for a second. Then I got it.

"Your weaselly bunkmate," I said. "Anton!"

Just then, someone leaned over my shoulder to look at the pictures. It was the strange old man.

"That Anton boy is trouble," the old man said, shaking his head. "Just take a look in that bag of tricks he has."

"How do you know about Anton?" I asked.

"I see things that other folks miss," the old man said.

Suddenly he looked worried. "I better skedaddle," he said. "Here comes Sheriff Bob Ian Grady!" Once again, the old man vanished.

THE BAG OF TRICKS

After lights out, once Eliza was asleep,
Cat and I snuck over to Gum and Egg's room.
We had to check Anton's bag.

Gum and Egg were still awake. We heard
Anton snoring before we even got inside.

Anton's bag was on the floor beside his
bed. Gum shined a flashlight so we could see.

Quietly, I pulled the zipper of Anton's bag
and stuck my hand in.

My fingers touched something weird.

It felt like a head!

"Shine the light in here," I whispered. "What is this?"

"Pull it out!" Cat said.

So I did. It wasn't a head at all. Just hair!

Egg whispered, "Why does Anton have a long wig?"

Then I pulled out something else. "Probably the same reason he has this giant hat," I said. "They're disguises."

"Is Anton the person in all the pictures?" Cat asked.

"Looks that way," I said. "He was trying to look like the deputy or the sheriff!"

Then I said louder, "Wake up, Anton, you little rat!"

Anton sat straight up. "Who's there?" he cried out.

"It's just us," I said. "It's time for you to confess."

"Yeah," Gum said. "You broke the porch."

"And you rigged that can of paint in the Saloon," Cat added.

"And you stole the ticket money!" Egg added.

"Whoa!" Anton replied. "I didn't take the money, I swear!"

"But you did do those other things?" I asked.

"Yes," Anton said. "I set up a couple of pranks. But I would never take money that didn't belong to me."

"That's hard to believe," I said. "Where were you when the money was stolen that first morning?"

"I was at the Saloon setting up the paint can trap," Anton said. "Honest! I don't steal!"

The four of us sat back. "He's telling the truth, I think," Cat said.

I nodded. "Okay," I said. "But why the hat and wig?"

Anton shrugged. "They're my normal disguises," he said. "I didn't know the sheriff would have long hair and the deputy would have a big hat."

"Just got lucky?" Gum asked.

"I guess," Anton replied. He yawned. "Can I go back to sleep now?"

The four of us laughed. "Good idea," Egg said. He walked over to his bed and lay down.

Cat and I quietly headed for the door. "I'm pooped anyway," I said.

But we still don't know who stole that money, I thought.

And time was running out.

CHAPTER ELEVEN

B.I.G. FINALE

From the second I fell asleep to the moment I woke up, my mind kept thinking about that stolen money.

I dreamed about dollar bills and camp tickets chasing me down Main Street. I turned onto First Street to try to get away, but they were waiting for me at the blacksmith's. I just couldn't escape.

So when I woke up the next morning, I was feeling pretty down and tired.

The field trip mystery crew never left a crime unsolved! Never! But it was our last day at Scrub Brush. There was no time left.

It was another hot, dry morning. Gum and Egg walked over to me and Cat as we left our room.

"Can you believe this?" Gum said.

"A crime going unsolved," I said, shaking my head.

"And now the camp will have to close," Cat added.

Feeling bad, the four of us climbed onto the bus. As we walked toward our favorite seats, I saw something on the floor of the bus. I bent over and picked up a wrapper from a BIG Burger.

"Who left their trash on the bus?" Cat said.

"That's pretty rude," Gum added.

"I agree," I said. "But it's also the last clue I needed! Come on, guys. I know who took the money!"

"Hey!" Mr. Spade called after us as we ran. "The bus is about to leave!"

But we couldn't stop now. In seconds, we were at the sheriff's office.

I burst through the door.

Sheriff Bob was on the phone. "The camp will have to close," he said into the phone. "With that money gone, the old man's broke." He laughed. "I'm sure he'll be ready to sell to BIG Stop now," he said.

"I knew it!" I said. "Sheriff Bob is none other than Bob Ian Grady. B.I.G.!"

"Big?" Egg said. "Oh! As in BIG Stop!"

The sheriff turned to us. The whole class, Mr. Spade, and Deputy Laurie were behind us at the door.

To my surprise, the sheriff didn't freak out or try to escape. Instead, he laughed.

"Yes," he said. "I am Bob Ian Grady, president of the BIG Stop Restaurant Corporation."

Deputy Laurie looked shocked. "I had no idea," she said.

"You mean that's not why you two were arguing?" I asked.

The deputy shook her head. "I was just mad he got the sheriff part instead of me," she said. "He doesn't even know how to lasso!"

"We thought you were in on it," I said.

Deputy Laurie gasped. "No way," she told me. "I never knew Bob was doing anything wrong."

"That man is a criminal," I said.

Mr. Grady laughed again. Then he said, "I own BIG Stop. But that's no crime."

"But it is a crime to steal the ticket money so the land will have to be sold to you!" I replied.

"You can't prove a thing," Mr. Grady replied. "Anyhow, you kids have a bus to catch. Thank you for visiting Scrub Brush. Now run along!"

The sheriff turned in his chair and pretended to ignore us. He wanted to go back to his phone call.

But just then, one more person came bursting into the sheriff's office.

It was the weird old man.

"We can prove it, Grady," the old man said. "I found this in the prospectors' tent by the brook."

He held up a leather bag. Then he turned it over. Piles of money fell onto the office floor.

"The ticket money!" Deputy Laurie said.

The sheriff shrugged. "So?" he said. "One of those actors who play the prospectors did it. You can't prove I had anything to do with it."

"Oh yes we can," Egg said. "I have a photo of you holding that bag and going into the tent. That's all the proof the real police will need."

"That and probably some fingerprints," I added.

Suddenly Sheriff Bob's face turned pale. He looked at the old man.

"How did you find that bag?" the fake sheriff asked. "No one uses those tents. They're just props! The actors have their own rooms."

"I'm no actor," said the old man. Then he pulled off his ragged hat and overcoat. "I have been sleeping in that tent all weekend, watching over this camp, and keeping this land safe!"

Suddenly I recognized him. "You're the man I saw at the BIG Stop on our way here, aren't you?" I asked. "Arguing with that businesswoman."

The man nodded. "That's right, young lady," he said. "That woman was Grady's assistant."

Egg scratched his chin. "Who are you?" he asked.

"Why, I'm Jeb Brush," the old man said. "I own this camp!"

Mr. Spade stepped forward and shook Mr. Brush's hand.

"Good to meet you, Mr. Brush," our teacher said. "Thanks to these crime-solving students, I guess you're going to own this camp a little longer."

Mr. Brush smiled and winked at my friends and me. "This camp will be around a long time," he said. "Thanks to these kids. But no thanks to Bob Ian Grady!"

I looked over at the fake sheriff. He was trying to climb out the window! "Stop him!" I yelled.

All of the kids in my class ran over and grabbed Mr. Grady.

Deputy Laurie put the sheriff in handcuffs. "I'm not a real deputy," she said. "But these are real handcuffs."

"You can't stop me," Mr. Grady said. "I'll own this land somehow!" I thought he looked like he was going to cry.

The deputy pulled the sheriff out of the office. "Explain it to the real cops," she told him.

"All right, class," Mr. Spade said. "Let's head home."

Mr. Spade led the class back to the bus. We all filed on.

Cat, Gum, Egg, and I sat in the very back row, like always.

The driver started up the engine and the bus slowly pulled away from the camp.

"Will we stop for a snack again, Mr. Spade?" the driver asked.

Mr. Spade looked at me, Cat, Gum, and Egg.

"Yes, we'll stop for a snack, Willy," he said.

"Just anywhere but BIG Stop!"

THE END

Dear parent/guardian of Catalina Duran,

Mr. Neff's science class is going on a field trip!

We'll be traveling to the River City Recycling Plant
to learn about recycling and the environment.

*We have been promised that no one will be trying to
sabotage the recycling plant while we're there.*

Please sign and return this form as soon as possible so
that your child will be allowed to attend the field trip.

Tom Duran

Parent/Guardian Signature

THE TEACHER WHO Forgot Too Much

Catalina Duran
A.K.A: Cat
D.O.B: February 15th
POSITION: 6th Grade

INTERESTS:
Animals, being "green", field trips

KNOWN ASSOCIATES:
Archer, Samantha; Garrison, Edward; and Shoo, James. *Are these students spending too much time together?*

NOTES:
Catalina is well liked by most of her teachers and fellow students. *Sounds like a troublemaker.*

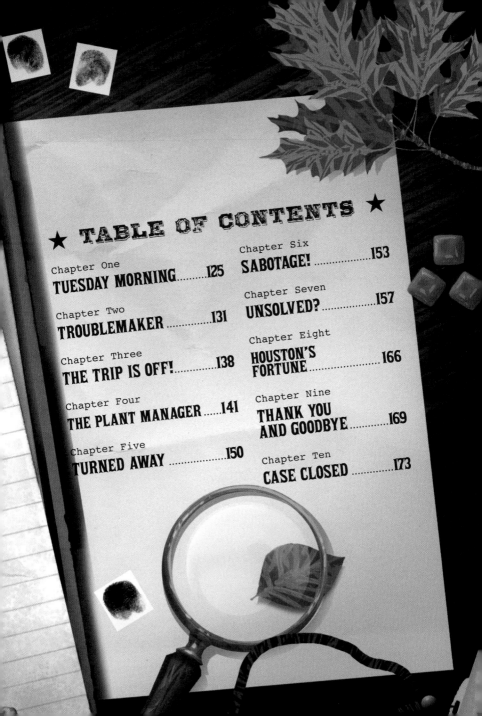

★ TABLE OF CONTENTS ★

TUESDAY MORNING

My name is Catalina Duran,

but everyone calls me Cat –

like the cute and fuzzy animal.

Not that I'm fuzzy.

Anyway, my best friends and I have been through some crazy days. The weird thing is what happens on field trip days.

Whenever we go on a field trip, it seems like something's always getting stolen or being wrecked or going missing. For some reason, my friends and I have a knack for solving these crimes!

The day I'm here to tell you about started out as a totally normal Tuesday morning.

Before school, I was sitting on the school's front steps with Gum.

Gum and I are usually the first of the bunch to get to school. We both live close to school, so we walk. It only takes me about five minutes, and Gum's walk isn't much longer.

"Is it Friday yet?" Gum asked.

I laughed and said, "It's only Tuesday, Gum. Not even close to Friday."

Just then, Sam and Egg's bus pulled up. The brakes made a very loud squeak. Gum and I both covered our ears.

Sam and Egg were the very last ones off the bus. They always sit together all the way in the back.

"Good morning, you two," Egg said. He pulled his camera to his eye and snapped a quick shot of me and Gum.

"Good morning," I replied.

Egg glanced at his watch. "Let's hurry up so we get to class," he said. "I don't want Mr. Neff to leave without us!"

"Leave without us?" I asked. "What are you talking about?"

"He really might!" Sam said. "Mr. Neff is so absentminded, he probably would forget us here if we were even one minute late."

Gum laughed. "Yeah," he said. "Remember that time he showed up in a suit, but forgot his shirt?"

I giggled. "He looked pretty funny with that jacket and tie on," I added.

A few minutes later, we were walking to Mr. Neff's science class.

We have science with Mr. Neff every Tuesday morning. Other mornings, we have different classes, like art or music or gym. The rest of the time we're in our regular class with Mr. Spade, our sixth-grade teacher.

Mr. Spade was leading us through the halls to Mr. Neff's science room. You could smell Mr. Neff's science room from miles away. It stinks like chemicals! I don't mind the smell though. I like science class. And I really like Mr. Neff.

Mr. Neff loves animals as much as I do, I think. Plus, he's always teaching us new ways to be green and to help the environment. He's even on some special city committee to make sure our town recycles and stays green.

One day he told us that he had helped the committee win a big lawsuit against the town landfill.

They had made it illegal for anything that could be recycled to go to the landfill. That meant our town had to recycle a lot of stuff instead of just throwing it away. I thought that was pretty cool.

"So," I said to Sam as we walked, "what was Egg talking about before? When he said that thing about Mr. Neff leaving without us?"

"Don't you remember, Cat?" Sam replied. "Field trip today!"

I thought for a moment. "Oh that's right!" I said. "The city recycling plant. I can't believe I forgot!"

Sam nodded. "Yup," she said. "I figured you'd be so excited."

"I am!" I replied. I really was. I don't know how I forgot. But this field trip to the recycling plant was a big deal for me.

Mr. Neff taught us a lot about recycling. He said that the world would be a better place if we didn't have to recycle — if we all stopped using stuff made out of plastic, and only used things that were biodegradable. But until then, he said, recycling was a great thing to do.

Like I said, I love animals. And anything that helps animals — which includes recycling — I also love.

So I was very excited when Sam reminded me about the trip.

"Do you think they'll show us how the plastic is recycled and used to make carpets?" I asked. "Oh, I hope so!"

The others shrugged.

"Maybe we'll see aluminum cans being melted into fresh aluminum," I added. "Aluminum is very easy to recycle. That would be amazing!"

My friends just looked at me. For some reason, they just didn't seem as excited as I was.

"Well, I don't care what you guys say," I finally said. "This is an awesome field trip!"

But I had no idea how exciting that field trip would actually be.

CHAPTER TWO

TROUBLEMAKER

"Okay, everyone," Mr. Neff said as the bus bounced along. "Let's take attendance so we know we're not missing anyone."

"Attendance now?" Gum whispered to me. The four of us were sitting in the two back seats. I was sitting in one seat with Gum, and Sam and Egg were across the aisle.

"What's the problem?" I asked.

"Isn't it too late if we did forget someone?" Gum said.

I laughed. "Yep," I said. "Plus, Mr. Neff can never remember our names anyway!"

Mr. Neff glanced around the bus. "I'll start in the back," he said, glancing at me and my friends.

Now, to be fair, we all love Mr. Neff. He's very nice and very funny. He is also the only teacher who uses our nicknames instead of our real names. That's pretty cool. The problem is, he can never remember what our nicknames are!

"Okay, Kit?" he said.
He was looking right at me.

No one replied.

"Um," Mr. Neff tried again, still looking at me. "Dog?"

I slowly raised my hand. "You mean Cat, Mr. Neff?" I asked.

Mr. Neff looked confused, but then he smiled. "That's right, Cat," he said.

"Here," I replied with a smile.

It went on like that for the rest of the ride. He called Gum "Candy," and Egg "Cheese," then "Milk." He did manage to get Sam's name right on the first try, though.

For the millionth time, Mr. Neff said, "Sorry about that, everyone. I'm great with faces, just awful with names!"

Just as the bus was pulling up to the recycling plant, a baseball hit the floor of the bus and bounced up to the front. It hit Mr. Neff right in the foot. Egg snapped a quick picture.

"Huh?" Mr. Neff said, bending over to get it. "What's this?"

"It's mine, Mr. Neff," Anton Gutman replied. He's the class meanie. He makes fun of everyone all the time. He's always causing trouble for the teachers.

"Why do you have a baseball with you, Andrew?" Mr. Neff asked, walking down the bus aisle to Anton's seat.

"Anton," Anton said, correcting him.

"Right," Mr. Neff said impatiently. "Why do you have a baseball?"

"Actually," Anton said, smiling, "I have three baseballs." He reached out and took the ball back from Mr. Neff.

"Why?" Mr. Neff asked. I could tell that he was getting annoyed.

"They're for our baseball game after school," Anton told him. "That one just fell out of my bag. It was an accident."

"Don't let it happen again," Mr. Neff said. Then the bus stopped. Everyone quickly stood up.

"Okay, everyone off," Mr. Neff announced.

We all got into a group on the sidewalk in front of the plant. Just then, a man came running out of the plant.

"The field trip is off!" the man yelled.

"What?" Mr. Neff asked. All of us students stood there, shocked.

"Sorry, everyone," the man replied. "No field trip! The city recycling plant is closed — maybe for good!"

THE TRIP IS OFF!

"We planned this field trip months ago," Mr. Neff said. "You can't cancel it now that we're here."

The man patted his sweaty forehead with a hanky. "Are you Mr. Neff, the science teacher?" he asked.

"That's right," Mr. Neff replied. "What is the problem exactly?" Mr. Neff peeked around the tall man to try to look inside the plant.

"Mr. Neff, I'm Joe Astor," the man said. He stuck out his hand and Mr. Neff shook it. "I'm the shift supervisor."

"It's nice to meet you, Mr. Astor," Mr. Neff replied. "I wish you'd tell me the problem."

"Well," Mr. Astor said, "several machines in the plant suddenly broke down this morning."

"Broke down?" Gum asked. "How?"

Mr. Astor glanced at Gum and shrugged. "We don't know," the supervisor said. "But our new manager is very angry. It's his first day working at the recycling plant, and everything is going wrong! I can't bring a class of sixth graders through right now."

Mr. Neff leaned forward and spoke more quietly. "Listen," he said. "Suppose we just take them through very quickly. They can see the machines, even if nothing is working."

Mr. Astor frowned. "I don't know," he said slowly.

"The new manager won't even know we're here," Mr. Neff said. He smiled slyly.

Mr. Astor thought a moment. "Okay," he said in a whisper. "I'll walk you through, but we have to be quick!"

The whole class cheered. Mr. Astor jumped about ten feet. "And quiet!" he shouted. "Tell your students to be quiet!"

CHAPTER FOUR

THE PLANT MANAGER

The class followed Mr. Neff and Mr. Astor as quietly as we could into the recycling plant. We walked into a big room. It had a couple of nice couches, and thick green carpeting. There were several closed doors. There were three desks in the room, too. Each one had a small computer on it. Each desk also had a person's name on it. One of them belonged to Mr. Astor.

The last student into the plant's lobby closed the front door very quietly.

"Thank you for letting us in, Mr. Astor," I whispered. I was right up in front.

The sweaty supervisor glanced at me and smiled. His face was bright red. I could see he was having a very bad day. "You're welcome, young lady," he replied in a whisper.

Mr. Astor looked up at the rest of the class. "This is the front office lobby area," he said in a slightly louder whisper. "We have to be very, very quiet in here," he added.

"How come?" Egg whispered, standing next to me. I'm sure no one else in the class heard him ask.

"The plant manager's office is right through that door," Mr. Astor replied in his quietest voice yet.

Mr. Astor pointed at a very fancy-looking wooden door across the room. It had golden trim and an engraved nameplate that said "Mr. Greenstreet."

Suddenly I heard someone giggling behind me. I glanced over my shoulder. Anton Gutman and two of his weaselly friends were standing together in the back of the group. They were laughing.

Sam leaned over to me, eyeing the group of troublemakers. "Thick as thieves, those three," she said.

Sam's always saying weird things like that. Half the time I don't have a clue what she's talking about. Gum and Egg and I always have to figure out what she means. But before I could ask what she meant, I heard a loud thud.

Behind us, Anton and his friends nearly fell over laughing. I looked around and spotted a baseball bouncing away from the manager's fancy office door. I guess that's what had made the loud noise.

The ball bounced right under Mr. Astor's desk. I doubt anyone but me and Sam even noticed it happen.

But everyone had heard the loud thud — including the plant manager.

Suddenly the fancy door flew open. A man came storming out. He was wearing a big hat and had a very funny mustache.

"What in the world was that?" he shouted angrily.

Then he stopped in his tracks. He had noticed the big group of sixth graders.

Mr. Astor tried to smile. I heard him swallow nervously.

The manager stood over us and looked at each of us, one by one. Quietly, Egg snapped a quick photo.

"Sir," Mr. Astor said. "This is Mr. Neff's sixth-grade class."

The manager stared at Mr. Astor.

Mr. Astor turned bright red.

"Their field trip is today," Mr. Astor added.

"That's right," Mr. Neff said. "We've been looking forward to it."

"Field trip," the manager muttered. "I see."

Then he glared at Mr. Neff. For a moment, I thought the manager would start shouting again. But instead, he suddenly smiled and quickly walked over to Mr. Neff.

"Mr. Neff!" the manager said very pleasantly. "Why, it's a pleasure to meet you!"

Mr. Neff smiled and shook the manager's hand. "The pleasure is mine," Mr. Neff said. "But I think we've met before. I just can't remember where."

The manager thought for a moment. "Really?" he asked.

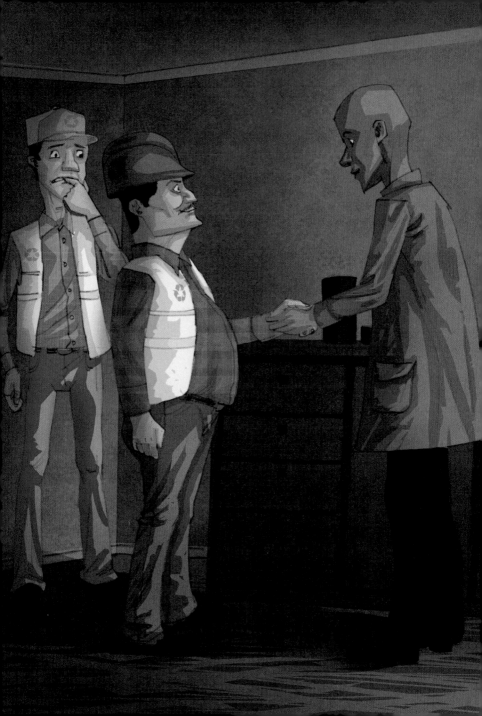

Mr. Neff nodded. "I'm certain," he said. "I never forget a face! Ask my class."

We all nodded to support our teacher. He was bad at names, but we all knew he was great at remembering faces.

"Mr. Dallas, isn't it?" Mr. Neff said.

The manager shook his head.

"Hmm, Mr. Austin, perhaps?" Mr. Neff tried again.

"Nope. My name is Mr. Greenstreet. And I don't think we've met before," the manager said.

Mr. Neff seemed confused. "I was sure it was Dallas or Austin," he muttered to himself. "Or maybe Arlington . . . ?"

"Well, enjoy your visit with us, class," Mr. Greenstreet said. "I need to get back to work. Oh, and did Mr. Astor tell you that most of the machines are broken? The plant isn't running today."

"Yes," Mr. Neff replied. "I'm sorry the kids won't see the plant in action."

Mr. Greenstreet shrugged. "Can't be helped," he said. With that, he walked back into his office. Then he slammed the door behind him.

TURNED AWAY

I have to say, the tour of the plant wasn't all that interesting. I mean, it was cool to see the piles of plastic here, and metal there, and paper over there. But with no machines whirring or materials being processed, there wasn't much to see.

Even the plant workers were mainly standing around. Egg took some photos of the stopped machines and the workers standing near them, but even Egg was bored. And he's **hardly ever bored** when he has his camera.

By the time lunch came along, we were all glad to go out to the picnic area and get some air. Mr. Neff stayed inside to talk to Mr. Astor.

"This is the worst field trip ever," Gum said as he unpacked his lunch. "What a waste of a day!"

Sam shrugged. "It's better than sitting in a hot classroom," she said.

"I guess," Gum agreed.

While we were eating our sandwiches, a loud truck pulled up at the loading bay nearby. Its engine chugged and sputtered to a stop. Then the driver hopped out.

Just then, Mr. Astor came jogging out of the loading bay door. "Hold it!" he cried. "Just a moment, please!"

"What's the problem, Joe?" the driver asked. He was ready to dump a big load of recyclables into the loading area. Then the bottles and cans and whatever else was in the truck would be sorted and brought inside the plant.

"We're too backed up in there," Mr. Astor said. "All of the machines have stopped working. We can't take any more recyclables today."

The driver scratched his head. "What am I supposed to do with this load?" he asked, pointing at his truck.

Mr. Astor took a deep breath and wiped the sweat from his brow. "I'm afraid you'll just have to take it all over to Houston's," he said.

The driver frowned. "Houston's Landfill? They don't take recyclables over there."

"Well, they do today," Mr. Astor said.

He quickly fanned his face with his hand. "Mr. Greenstreet arranged it."

"If you say so," the driver said. He got back into his truck and started it up. "I'll see you soon, Joe."

Mr. Astor waved. Then the big truck drove off.

SABOTAGE!

By the time the noise of the loud truck
driving away faded, lunch was over.

"Okay, class," Mr. Neff said, coming
outside. "We're going to head back to school
now."

"All good things must come to an end,
I guess," Sam said.

The four of us got up from our table and
tossed our empty wrappers into a nearby
trashcan.

Then, as we went back into the plant to
leave through the front door, Mr. Astor
came running toward us. He was holding
something in his hand.

"Stop!" he shouted at us. "Don't you kids leave yet!"

Mr. Neff turned. "What is it, Mr. Astor?" he asked.

Mr. Astor ran up to us and caught his breath. "Look what the maintenance crew just found in one of our broken machines!" he yelled.

He held up a baseball. It was badly scarred and torn up, but it was definitely a baseball.

Egg quickly snapped a photo of the torn-up ball.

Mr. Neff frowned at Mr. Astor. "I hope you're not suggesting one of my students had something to do with the broken machines!" Mr. Neff said.

Mr. Astor gasped. "I certainly am," he said. "The machine in question was one of the few that was actually working fine before your students got here."

Mr. Neff turned and faced Anton. "Andrew," Mr. Neff said, "Did you throw a baseball into a machine?"

"My name is Anton!" the troublemaker replied. "And no, I didn't."

Gum stepped up to Anton. "We all saw your baseball, Anton," Gum said. "It had to be you!"

"Let me see your bag," Mr. Neff said to Anton. He grabbed Anton's bag.

Anton looked around. "Okay," he said.

Mr. Neff reached in and soon pulled out two baseballs. "Where's the third one?" he asked.

Anton smiled. "What third one?" he said smugly.

"On the bus you told me you had three baseballs for your game after school," Mr. Neff replied. "So where's the third?"

Anton shrugged. "I must have been wrong," he said. "I guess I only had two."

"He's lying!" Mr. Astor said. He held up the torn-up baseball. Then he said, "This is the third one! That boy sabotaged our machine."

"You're going to be in big trouble when we get back to school, young man," Mr. Neff told Anton. "Unless you can show me where that third baseball is, I'm afraid I can't think of any other explanation!"

CHAPTER SEVEN

UNSOLVED?

Sam and I glanced at each other.

"**I can't believe** we're about to do this," I said.

"I know," Sam agreed. "We're going to clear Anton Gutman's name."

We both shook our heads, but we had to be honest.

"Mr. Neff," I said. "Anton did have three baseballs."

"But the one Mr. Astor has isn't one of them," Sam added.

"What? What are you girls talking about?" Mr. Neff asked.

Egg and Gum glanced at us. "Yeah," Gum said, "what are you two talking about?"

"We'll show you," I replied. I took Sam by the arm. Together, we walked into the lobby. Mr. Neff and Mr. Astor followed us, and the rest of the class followed them.

"It went under there," Sam said. She pointed to Mr. Astor's desk.

I got down on all fours near the desk. I reached around under the desk, but I couldn't find anything. I scooched down as far as I could and reached as far back under the desk as I could.

Nothing.

"I don't get it," I said, jumping to my feet. "That's where the ball went."

Anton walked up. "Um, didn't you find it?" he asked, looking at me.

I shrugged and shook my head.

Sam got down on her knees and looked under the desk. "I'm sure that's where it went," she said. "I saw it roll under there!"

"It did!" Anton said. He looked worried. "I saw it!"

"Weird," Sam said. I nodded. How could a baseball just disappear?

Anton spun to face Mr. Neff. "I swear, Mr. Neff," he said. "That's the last time I saw the third baseball."

"What is this all about?" Mr. Neff asked, looking confused. "What are we searching for?" He looked at me and Sam.

I glanced at Sam. We might not like Anton Gutman, but we're not tattlers. I didn't want to tell Mr. Neff what Anton had done with the ball before it rolled under there.

I looked at Anton. He swallowed.

I waited.

Anton swallowed again.

"Oh, hurry up," Sam said. "Come on!"

"Mr. Neff," Anton finally said, "I did have another baseball. When we first got here, I threw it at the manager's office door. Then it rolled under that desk, like Cat and Sam said."

Mr. Neff frowned. "Why did you do that?" he asked Anton.

Anton shrugged and looked at his feet. Usually, his pranks never got found out. He always got away with everything. Now, he looked pretty upset. "It was just a joke," he replied. "I thought it would be funny."

"Well, it wasn't funny," Mr. Neff said. He turned to Mr. Astor. "I'll deal with my students, Mr. Astor," Mr. Neff told him. "But unfortunately, anyone could have picked up that baseball after Andrew lost it."

"My name isn't Andrew. It's Anton," Anton said, correcting Mr. Neff.

"Right," Mr. Neff said. "I'm sorry Anton brought that baseball into your plant, Mr. Astor, but it seems he knows nothing about the sabotage."

Mr. Astor huffed and puffed. His face turned redder and redder. "Well, someone has broken our machines!" he said angrily, shaking his fist at us. "And I am going to find out who it was!"

With that, the supervisor stormed back into the main part of the plant.

Mr. Neff turned and looked at us. I could tell he was very disappointed.

"Do you think we should get back on the bus, Mr. Neff?" Egg asked.

Mr. Neff glanced at his watch. "It's earlier than we were supposed to leave," he said. "I better call the bus driver to let him know we're ready to head back. You kids stay here in the lobby." He walked off to make the call.

"So who do you guys think sabotaged the machines?" Sam asked.

Gum stroked his chin. "I'll solve this mystery," he said. "Just give me a minute."

Egg looked around to make sure no one was listening. Then he said, "I think it was Mr. Neff."

"Mr. Neff?" I said, practically shouting. "Are you crazy?"

Egg shook his head. "No, I'm not crazy. Don't you remember what he said in class?" he asked.

"You mean that he hates plastics?" Sam asked.

Egg nodded. "Right," he said. "If the recycling plant stops working, people might stop using plastic. Since Mr. Neff said it's illegal for the landfill to take recyclable stuff, then people would have to use things that could go to the landfill."

"Things that are biodegradable, you mean," I said.

"Right," said Egg.

"I don't know," Gum said. "I mean, today Houston's Landfill is taking recyclables."

"That's true," I said.

"Maybe they're just storing them and they'll bring them back when the recycling plant opens again, but I doubt it," Gum went on. "And I bet if the recycling plant was closed for good, it wouldn't be illegal to bring plastic to the landfill."

I added, "Mr. Neff seems to be glad we can recycle the plastic things, even if he doesn't much like them to begin with."

Egg put up his hands. "I still think it's Mr. Neff," he said. "He seems so distracted, and he has the motive. Stop the recycling plant so people can't use plastic."

"Mr. Neff always seems distracted," I said. "That's nothing new."

"I'm still not ruling out Anton," Gum said. "Just because he dropped the baseball doesn't mean he didn't go back later and pick it up."

"The baseball was under Mr. Astor's desk," I pointed out. "Maybe he found it."

Just then, Mr. Neff came back into the lobby. "Okay, class," he said. "The bus will be out front in a moment. Let's head out there and get in line, please."

"I guess we're not going to solve this mystery," I said sadly.

"But we have to solve it!" Gum said as we headed out the front door. "We always solve the mysteries!"

Sam sighed. "We don't even have one clue," she said. "How can we?"

That moment, another loud truck chugged up to the plant.

Mr. Astor ran outside. "Stop!" he shouted at the driver. "Don't pull that truck in. The plant is not accepting any materials today. The machinery has been sabotaged."

"The plant's been sabotaged?" the driver asked, shocked.

Mr. Astor nodded. "That's right," he said. "So until we find out who broke the machines, everything has to go to Houston's Landfill instead."

"Houston's Landfill," I said quietly. "I wonder . . ."

CHAPTER EIGHT

HOUSTON'S FORTUNE

"Mr. Astor!" I said, jogging over to him. "Can I ask you a question?"

The driver of the recycling truck went back to his truck. Mr. Astor turned to me and wiped his brow.

"What is it, young lady?" Mr. Astor said. "I'm very busy."

"Well," I said quickly, "how come Houston's Landfill is taking all the recycling?"

"Where else would it go?" he replied. "It can't fit in the plant with the machines broken. And the drivers can't keep it on the trucks."

Egg stepped up beside me. "But Mr. Neff told us that landfills are not allowed to accept recyclables," he added.

"Right," I said. "It would be like putting a tin can in your compost pile!"

Mr. Astor looked at his watch. Then he glanced over at a nearby window. We saw Mr. Greenstreet, the plant manager, watching us.

"I don't have time to stand here and chat about it. Since the recycling plant is closed, the city made a deal with the landfill," Mr. Astor said.

"What kind of deal?" I asked.

"Houston's Landfill will take the recyclables until the recycling plant is up and running again," Mr. Astor said. "The city agreed to make it legal again and to pay double their normal fee. Mr. Houston must be making a fortune today!" He shook his head and walked off.

"Double their fee?" Egg said, shocked.

"And it's not illegal for them to take recyclables anymore," I said. "I think we found our motive."

Sam and Gum walked up to us.

"We have to get on the bus," Sam said.

"Tell Mr. Neff to wait," I said. "I think we just solved this mystery."

CHAPTER NINE

THANK YOU AND GOODBYE

"Kit!" Mr. Neff said. "Cheese! The bus needs to leave now. We're waiting for you."

I laughed. "It's Cat and Egg!" I said.

"Not Kit and Cheese!"

"I can't keep track of these crazy names," Mr. Neff said. "But we have to get on the bus now."

"Just one minute, Mr. Neff," I said. "I want to say thank you and goodbye to the plant manager."

I rushed back into the lobby and knocked on Mr. Greenstreet's door.

"We don't have time for this, Kitty!" Mr. Neff said as he ran after me. "Leave Mr. Arlington alone!"

Egg jogged up next to me. "What are you up to, Cat?" he asked. "I don't think Mr. Greenstreet wants to be bugged right now. He seemed so angry before."

"I think Mr. Neff was closer when he said Arlington," I replied. "Or Dallas or Austin."

"Huh?" Mr. Neff said. "What's she talking about, Biscuit?" he asked Egg.

I banged on the office door again. Finally, it swung open.

"What is it?" the manager shouted. His mustache looked crooked.

"Sorry to bother you, Mr. Houston," I said, smiling. "I just wanted to thank you for letting us visit."

"Yes, yes," the manager replied. His belly shook. "Don't mention it. Goodbye."

"Mr. Houston!" Mr. Neff suddenly shouted. "That's it! I knew we'd met before."

"What?" the manager said in a huff. "No, no. My name is Greensleeves. I mean, Greenstreet."

"Aha!" Egg said. "You're Mr. Houston, the owner of Houston's Landfill."

Mr. Neff frowned. "That's right," our teacher said. "I met you at the community board meeting. That's when we made it illegal for your landfill to accept any recyclables!"

He looked hard at the man and added angrily, "And your mustache is fake!"

The manager grumbled and started to say something, but instead he just stepped back into his office and closed the door. I heard the latch drop as he locked it from the inside.

Mr. Neff put a hand on my shoulder. "You sure cracked that case, Rabbit," he said.

Egg, or should I say "Cheese," and I laughed.

CHAPTER TEN

CASE CLOSED

Detective Jones showed up pretty quickly after Mr. Astor called the police.

"You kids again!" the detective said when he saw me, Egg, Gum, and Sam. "I think I'll have to make you honorary detectives before long," he added. "Who solved this one?"

Egg pointed at me. "It was Cat," he said.

The detective looked at me. "So how did you figure it out?" he asked. "How did you know Mr. Greenstreet, the new plant manager, was actually Mr. Houston, the owner of Houston's Landfill, in disguise?"

"Well," I replied, "Mr. Neff really deserves the credit."

"Me?" Mr. Neff said. "What did I do?"

"You never get a name right," I said, "but you're always close!"

"Really?" Mr. Neff said, blushing. "I didn't know I did that."

"Sure," Egg said. "You call me 'Cheese' instead of 'Egg.'"

"And me 'Candy' instead of 'Gum,'" Gum added.

Sam and I laughed. "So," I went on, "when you called Mr. Greenstreet 'Dallas,' 'Austin,' and 'Arlington' . . ."

"All cities in Texas!" Sam pointed out.

I nodded. "Just like Houston," I finished, "the name of the landfill that is making extra money today because of the broken equipment! That's how I figured out that Mr. Houston did it."

The detective nodded slowly. "Brilliant work," he said. "You'll make a fine addition to the force some day."

With that, he led Mr. Houston out of the lobby and into a police car.

"Another mystery solved," Gum said, clapping his hands together.

"And more importantly," I said, picking up a plastic water bottle from the ground, "Mr. Houston won't be able to stop this city from recycling."

Mr. Neff patted me on the back. "Good going, Cat," he said. "Or is it Puppy?"

The four of us laughed as our teacher stepped onto the bus.

"Think he'll get our names right before we finish the school year?" Sam asked.

"Not a chance, Pam," I said. "Not a chance."

Dear parent/guardian of Edward Garrison,

The science club is going on a field trip!

We'll be traveling to the River City Zoo to see the special Island Foxes exhibit, because we've been learning about endangered species.

We are sure that no one will try to kidnap the Island Foxes while we are there.

Please sign and return this form as soon as possible so that your child will be allowed to attend the field trip.

Jerome Garrison
Parent/Guardian Signature

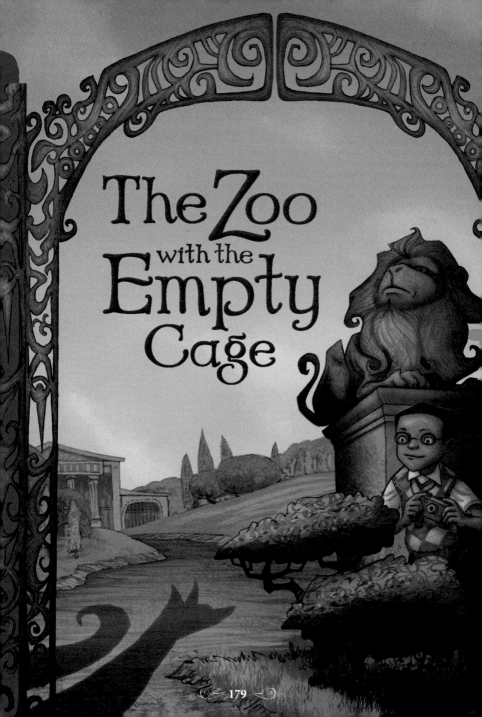

The Zoo with the Empty Cage

Edward G. Garrison
A.K.A: Egg
D.O.B: May 14th
POSITION: 6th Grade

*This can't be correct.
Please confirm.*

INTERESTS:
Photography, field trips
KNOWN ASSOCIATES:
Archer, Samantha; Duran, Catalina;
and Shoo, James.
NOTES:
Ms. Stanwyck encourages Edward's
passion for photography, but some
teachers complain of the frequent
use of the flash.

*Is photography allowed in school? I will
look into this.*

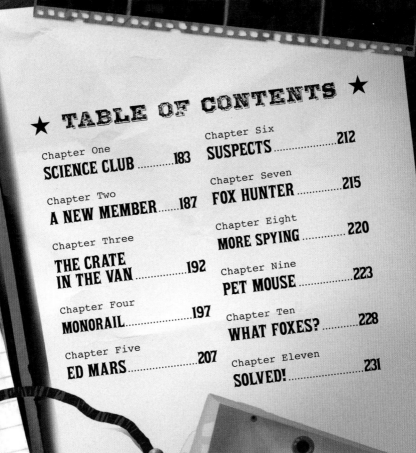

★ TABLE OF CONTENTS ★

CHAPTER ONE

SCIENCE CLUB

My name is
Edward G. Garrison,
but you can call me Egg.

Yup, Egg. Like the things you scramble for breakfast. Anton Gutman, our class bully, says people call me Egg because my brain is scrambled, but he's wrong. It's just my initials: E.G.G.

That's why my friends call me Egg.

My best friends, Gum, Sam, and Cat, and I are the closest friends in sixth grade. It feels like we've been friends forever. But we only met this year in science club, actually.

Cat is the only one of us who really likes science. She's a big-time animal lover, and science is the only class where we learn about animals. Cat joined the science club because she wanted to take care of the club's gerbil, Mr. Herbert.

Sam loves all those police shows on TV. You know, the ones where special cops solve crimes using science. So she joined the science club hoping to learn how to take DNA samples or something. She says that's called forensic science.

The science club member who really doesn't fit is Gum. He completely hates science class. In fact, the only reason he joined at all is because Mr. Neff, the science teacher, made him join.

See, Gum was causing trouble on the first day of science class this year. The punishment was to join the science club for at least a month. Once Gum became friends with the rest of us, he decided to stay.

And why did I join? Extra credit! Every member of the science club gets extra credit on our science grades at the end of year.

I'm going to need it. I'm always busy taking pictures during class, so I often miss what Mr. Neff, the science teacher, is trying to teach. Science isn't my favorite subject. Art is. I love photography.

But science club isn't just where we all met. It's also the scene of one of our biggest mysteries ever. See, my friends and I solve a lot of mysteries. Most of them happen when we go on field trips.

This really big mystery started one Wednesday. That's the day that science club always meets.

Gum, Sam, Cat, and I were seated at the round table in the science room.

We were a few minutes early, and our new club advisor, Ms. Marlow, wasn't there yet. None of us knew Ms. Marlow very well. She had only started a week earlier.

"So, what do you guys think about Ms. Marlow?" Sam asked in a whisper.

Cat smiled. "I like her," she said. "Did you see her T-shirt last week?"

Gum laughed. "You mean the one with the panda bear on it?" he said. "I knew you'd like her."

Cat nodded. "Of course I do," she agreed. "That panda bear is the logo of a group that protects animals, and I love animals."

I got up and snapped a quick shot of my three friends at the round table. They all smiled. They're great photography subjects.

Just then, the door to the science room opened. We all turned, expecting to see Ms. Marlow.

Instead, we saw our arch nemesis.

Anton Gutman.

A NEW MEMBER

"Anton!" Gum said. He jumped out of his seat. "What are you doing here?"

"This is the science club meeting," Sam added.

"And we all know you don't like science," Cat pointed out.

Anton smirked. "I like science," he said. "In fact, I love science. It's my favorite subject."

Anton took a chair and pulled it over to the big round table. He flipped it around and sat in it backward.

"So," he said, "let's talk about planets or bugs or something."

Cat said, "Anton, stop goofing around. Ms. Marlow will be here any minute."

"I'm not goofing around," Anton insisted. "I'm joining the science club."

None of us could believe it. Anton Gutman was a troublemaker and a cheater. Why would he want to join the science club?

But before we could figure out what Anton was up to, Ms. Marlow strolled into the room. "Hello, students," she said.

"Hi, Ms. Marlow," Cat replied. "Um, where is Mr. Herbert? I'm supposed to feed him and water him. Plus, I have to clean his cage today."

Ms. Marlow turned to Cat. "Are you in charge of the gerbil?" Ms. Marlow asked.

"I didn't realize," she went on. "I brought him to my apartment to care for him."

Cat's shoulders sagged. "You took him home?" she asked.

Ms. Marlow smiled. "I did. I'm sorry, Catalina," she said. "It just broke my heart to think of Mr. Herbert at school by himself at night."

Cat nodded, but I could tell she was sad about it. She really liked that gerbil.

"I'll bring Mr. Herbert in on Wednesdays for science club from now on," Ms. Marlow added quickly. "You can visit with him then. And maybe you could take him on a weekend sometime. Would that be nice?"

"Yes," Cat replied. "That would be nice."

"Anyway," Ms. Marlow went on, "I have two pieces of news today. First, we have a new member."

Anton leaned back and stretched.

"Do you all know Anton?" Ms. Marlow asked. She frowned. "Anton will be with us for the next four weeks because he's having some trouble in science class."

Anton laughed.

"I knew you weren't here because you wanted to be," I said, leaning toward Anton. "This is a punishment!"

Anton smirked.

"I hope my other piece of news will cheer you up, Catalina," Ms. Marlow went on.

Cat sat up straight.

"As you know, the science club goes on a field trip every year," Ms. Marlow said. "This year, we'll have a special treat. We're going to the zoo!"

Cat squealed. "Yes!" she said.

Ms. Marlow smiled at Cat. Then she continued, "And even more exciting, we'll be the first to see a special new exhibit. The zoo recently got two Island Foxes."

Gum raised his hand. "I heard about that," he said. "They're — what do you call it? Engaged."

Cat laughed. "Not engaged," she said. "That means getting married. Island Foxes are endangered!"

Cat reached into her bag and pulled out a magazine. She flipped through the pages.

"Look," she said. She held up a photo of two animals. "These are Island Foxes. Cute, aren't they?"

Ms. Marlow nodded. "They are cute," she said. "The two at the zoo were recently captured in the wild."

Sam raised her hand. "Don't some zoos help endangered animals?" she asked.

Ms. Marlow nodded. "Yes," she said. "Some zoos capture animals to keep them safe and help them have babies."

Anton leaned over Cat's shoulder. "They look like ugly dogs to me," he said. "With funny short legs."

"It says here that Island Foxes live in California," Cat said. "They eat bugs, mice, fruit, and lizards. Gross!"

Anton laughed. "This isn't a very good punishment!" he said. "I get to go on a field trip."

Great, I thought. *The best field trip of the year, and Anton's coming.*

But the trouble hadn't even started yet.

CHAPTER THREE

THE CRATE IN THE VAN

The real excitement started the next week.
The next Wednesday, after the three o'clock
bell rang, the science club members met in front
of the school.

"Where's the bus?" Gum
asked, looking around.

I shrugged. "It's not here yet, I guess," I said.
The four of us looked up and down the street.
No bus.

Just then, a big white van pulled up. Ms.
Marlow hopped out of the driver's seat.

"Okay, kids," she said. "Let's head out to
the zoo."

We all turned and stared at Ms. Marlow. Quickly, I snapped a photo of the van.

"Um, are we going in that?" I asked.

Gum looked at me. "Don't we usually go on field trips in a bus?" he whispered.

"Yeah, usually," I said.

Ms. Marlow opened the sliding door of the van. "Sorry, kids," she said. "I know you prefer the hot and uncomfortable bus."

She gestured for us to climb into the van. Then she said, "Today, you'll have to enjoy the air-conditioned comfort of my personal eight-passenger luxury van. Climb in!"

Gum ran forward. "All right!" he shouted, climbing in. "Whoa, a TV!"

The rest of us shrugged and followed him into the van. It really was a nice van. The seats were leather and there was a TV with a DVD player and video game player. It was way cooler than any other van I'd ever been in.

"Since we're such a small group, the principal thought it would be a good idea to just take my van," Ms. Marlow explained.

I looked around. "Where's Anton?" I asked.

We looked out the window. Anton came running down the steps of the school. "Hold on!" he yelled. "I'm coming."

"You're a real piece of work, Gutman," Sam said when he got into the van. Sam watches a lot of old movies, so she says weird things sometimes.

"Whatever," Anton said.

"Hey, Ms. Marlow," Cat said. "What is the big crate in the back for?"

I turned in my seat. Way in the back of the van was a big metal crate.

"I have a very big dog, Catalina," Ms. Marlow replied. "That's where he sits when we go on long drives."

"Locked up in a cage?" Cat asked. "Poor guy!"

Ms. Marlow laughed nervously. "Yes, I know," she said. "I hate it too. But if I don't put him in there, he comes up front and tries to sit in my lap. It's very dangerous."

The trip in Ms. Marlow's van was awesome. We watched TV, played video games, and had a great time the whole way. It felt like the quickest trip ever. Before we knew it, we were at the zoo.

CHAPTER FOUR

MONORAIL

"Whoa, look at that!" Cat said when we got out of the van. She pointed up toward the sky over the zoo.

I turned to look. Right away, I picked up my camera. That was worth a photo. It was like a train from the future, soaring over the whole zoo!

"Pretty crazy, isn't it?" Ms. Marlow said. "The zoo spent millions on that new monorail."

Gum shielded his eyes and stared at the monorail. "It is pretty cool," he said.

Cat scratched her head. "Millions?" she asked. "That seems like a lot."

Ms. Marlow nodded. "It is a lot," she agreed. "The zoo could have spent it on improving some of these animals' living spaces."

I glanced at Cat. From the look on her face, I could tell Ms. Marlow's words made her feel sad.

"Are you okay, Cat?" I asked quietly.

Cat nodded. "Yeah," she said. "I just always thought this zoo was pretty good for the animals."

I wanted to say something, but I wasn't sure how to make her feel better.

Just then, a woman in tan shorts and a tan shirt came over to us. She looked like she just got back from a safari. "Hello, kids!" the woman said. "Is this the science club? I'm Shari, your guide. And I have a treat for you."

Cat stepped forward. "Island Foxes?" she asked excitedly.

Shari laughed. "Soon," she replied. "First, though, we'll have a superspeed tour of the zoo."

"Superspeed?" I asked. "Were we supposed to bring our running shoes?" I took a quick picture of Shari.

Shari smiled at me. "Of course not," she replied. "We'll be seeing everything from above, from the new monorail!"

"Yes!" Anton said. "That thing is so awesome."

Gum nodded. "For once, I have to agree with you, Anton," he said. "This is way cool."

Of course, I agreed. I mean, imagine the pictures you could take from up there. But when I looked at Cat and Ms. Marlow, I could see that not everyone was pleased.

"It'll be fun, Cat," I said as we followed Shari to the monorail entrance.

Cat shrugged. "I guess so," she replied. "I just feel bad if the zoo really did use money that could have helped the animals."

Soon we were high above the zoo. Cat sat next to Ms. Marlow. "Ms. Marlow," Cat said, "I thought this zoo was good for the animals. Don't most of the animals have lots of room to run and play?"

The monorail glided over a big expanse of grass and trees and hills. A golden lion was lounging in the grass. He seemed very relaxed and happy. I took a photo, of course.

Suddenly Gum jumped to his feet. He shouted, "Look at that!"

"Please stay seated," Shari said. We all looked out the window, trying to see what Gum was shouting about.

A huge group of people was marching around in front of the zoo. They were carrying signs and chanting. We couldn't hear what they were saying, though.

"Who are they?" I asked.

"Those are protestors," Ms. Marlow said. "It looks like the Animal Protectors, or the AP."

"You know them, Ms. Marlow?" Cat asked. She sounded like she wished she could join them.

"Yes," Ms. Marlow said. "When I was in college, I was the head of my local chapter of the AP."

"Not anymore?" I asked. I turned in my seat to take a few pictures of the protestors.

Ms. Marlow shook her head. "No," she said. "I left the group after college. It took up too much of my time."

"What are they protesting?" Sam asked.

The monorail took a sharp curve. Ms. Marlow pointed down to the gorilla area.

"My guess is they're protesting things like that cage," Ms. Marlow said. "See that big gorilla?"

We all looked down. A few gorillas were gathered on a small hill near a fake pond. The hill was surrounded on all sides by a heavy fence-like cage.

In the middle of the hill was the biggest gorilla. He had a gray back. The other gorillas were all black.

"That big one," Ms. Marlow said, "is a silverback. That means he's the oldest and strongest male. He's the leader."

"He's huge," Anton said. "Why is he just sitting there? Shouldn't he be beating his chest or something?"

Cat rolled her eyes. "Gorillas only do that if another gorilla is challenging them, or if there's danger," she said. "That gorilla isn't being challenged."

Shari smiled. "That's right!" she said. "I see we have an animal lover here."

Cat beamed. "I really love animals," she said.

Ms. Marlow frowned. "I wish whoever built that cage loved animals," she said quietly.

"What's wrong with the gorilla cage?" I asked. "They look happy and relaxed."

Ms. Marlow shook her head slowly. "To me they look sad and bored," she said. "Look at the size of the cage."

"Is it too small?" Cat asked.

The monorail began to slow down. It was pulling into a station.

"Much too small," Ms. Marlow replied. "One troop of gorillas in the wild should have a territory as big as twenty-five square miles."

"Wow," Gum said. "That's as big as . . ."

"This whole zoo," Cat suggested.

"Bigger than that," Sam added.

The monorail screeched to a halt.

We all started to get off. Then Ms. Marlow and Shari led us off the platform. "Actually, our entire town is about twenty-five square miles," Ms. Marlow said.

Shari smiled nervously. "Anyway," she said, "let's head to the Island Foxes!"

"Finally!" Cat said. I could tell she was excited to see the foxes.

Of course, when my friends and I go on a field trip, nothing is ever what we expect.

ED MARS

We followed close behind Shari and Ms. Marlow. Cat, Sam, and Gum huddled around me as we walked. I was looking through the pictures I'd taken from the monorail.

There were pictures of the gorillas, and some of the lions. Plus, I had gotten some great shots of the protestors.

Sam grabbed my hand. "Wait a second, Egg," she said. "Go back to that last photo."

I clicked the back button on my camera.

"That one!" Sam said. "Who is that?"

It was a picture of an older man. He was balding, but had a long gray ponytail. He was wearing a dirty red T-shirt and waving a sign.

"I don't know," I replied. "He's a protestor, I guess."

Sam stroked her chin. "I know that mug from someplace," she said. "Mug means face," she added quickly.

She thought a minute. Suddenly, she snapped her fingers. "That is Ed Mars," she said. "He's a famous animal rights protestor. I read about him in a magazine."

Ms. Marlow stopped walking. "Ed Mars?" she said. "Was he at the protest?"

Sam nodded. "I'm pretty sure it was him," she said.

Ms. Marlow said, "Wow. He's an idol of mine, in a way. He's done great things for animals over the years."

Sam frowned. "Wasn't he arrested recently?" she asked. "I think my grandpa was watching it on the news last week."

Ms. Marlow waved her hand. "Yes," she said. "Ed got in trouble for breaking into a laboratory and rescuing some monkeys."

Cat looked very upset to hear about the monkeys in the laboratory. But just then, Shari came to a sudden stop.

"Uh-oh," Shari said. "This doesn't look good."

We all jogged up to gather around Shari.

"What's going on?" Sam asked.

We were at the Island Fox exhibit, but no other visitors were around. Instead, it was swarming with zookeepers and police!

I snapped a few pictures right away.

Shari walked over to a man in a tan zoo uniform like hers. He was talking to the police.

When he saw Shari, the man shook his head. "This is bad, Shari," the zookeeper said.

"What happened?" our guide asked. "Aren't the foxes okay?"

The man took a deep breath. "I'm afraid I don't know," he said.

Shari looked confused. "What do you mean?" she asked. "Aren't we opening the exhibit today? These students are from the middle school science club. They're here to see the foxes."

The zookeeper sighed. "They won't see them today," he said. "The foxes have been stolen!"

CHAPTER SIX

SUSPECTS

Ms. Marlow and Shari went to talk to the police. They sent us to the snack stand. On our way, Cat, Gum, Sam, and I had our picture taken with a goat. Then we sat around a white plastic table.

We were all enjoying some ice cream. Gum's chewing gum was safely stored on the end of his nose to finish after the snack.

It didn't take long for Sam to come up with a suspect.

"I guess we all know who the foxnapper is," she said.

"We do?" Cat asked. "I have no idea who the foxnapper is."

Gum nodded slowly. "Of course we do!" he said. "It's so obvious."

I thought about it for a second. Who could it have been?

Then it hit me. "Aha!" I said. "It must have been Ed Mars."

Cat frowned. "I don't know," she said slowly.

"Why not?" I asked. "Sam said he had been arrested before for monkeynapping."

Sam shook her head. "No, no," she said. "I don't think it was Ed Mars."

I was shocked. "You don't?" I asked. "But he's the perfect suspect."

"I know who it is," Gum said. "I'm sure of it."

Sam cut him off. "It was Ms. Marlow," she said.

We all practically fell over. "Ms. Marlow?" Cat cried. "Are you serious?"

Sam smiled. "I'm sure of it," she said. "She obviously hates this zoo."

She did seem to hate it. "Do you think she took the Island Foxes so that she can free them?" I asked.

Sam nodded. "Plus," she went on, "she has that huge crate in her van."

Cat shook her head. "That's for her dog," she said. "She told us!"

"A likely story," Sam replied. "I don't believe it."

Gum said, "Maybe it was Ed Mars, and maybe it was Ms. Marlow, but I doubt it."

"Who do you think it was?" I asked.

"Who's missing from this table?" Gum replied.

Cat, Sam, and I looked around. "This is all of us," Cat said.

It wasn't all of us. "Anton!" I said, jumping to my feet. "Anton Gutman is missing!"

FOX HUNTER

Gum finished his ice cream and started chewing his gum again. "Anton is missing. The foxes are missing," he said. "Anton must have taken them."

"But why would Anton want the foxes?" I asked. "Ed Mars and Ms. Marlow both seem to have motives."

Gum shook his head. "Anton Gutman **never needs a motive,**" he said.

Cat nodded. "His motive is being a pain," she said. "Ed Mars and Ms. Marlow love animals. They wouldn't steal the foxes."

Gum pointed at Cat. "She's right," he said. "The foxes are being helped here."

We sat quietly and thought about it. Soon we heard some adults talking.

"Listen," Sam whispered. She's great at spying.

I glanced over. A few feet from us, two adults were talking loudly.

One of the adults was a woman. She was wearing a zoo uniform.

The other person was an older man. He had a big white mustache, and he was wearing glasses and a huge cowboy hat.

The man was saying, "I don't care if the foxes were stolen. I still have to get paid."

"I understand that," the woman replied. "You'll get your check."

"The full amount," the man said. His face was red with anger. "Five thousand dollars each!"

"Please, Mr. Moreno," the woman replied. "There's no reason to be upset."

The man took a deep breath. "I apologize for yelling," he said. "But this is my job, ma'am. I caught those foxes with my bare hands." Mr. Moreno took off his hat and wiped his forehead. "I'm sorry the foxes were stolen. But I must get paid for the work I did."

The woman nodded. "Come with me to the accounting office," she said. "We'll get you your check right away."

The two adults headed toward a small building. A sign on its door read "Employees Only."

"Did you hear that?" Sam whispered. "That was the hunter who captured the Island Foxes."

"Did you hear how much they pay him for that?" Gum added. "Five thousand dollars for one little fox. I think I'll become an animal hunter."

"He really wanted that check," Sam said.

I shrugged. "Well, like he said, it's his job," I replied.

Sam looked at me. "True," she said. "Come on. Let's go see what Ms. Marlow and Shari are doing."

We got up to head back to the fox exhibit. Just then, we saw Detective Jones hurry past.

"Hey, Detective Jones!" I called out.

He stopped and looked back. "Oh, hey," he said, waving. "My junior detectives. Are you trying to find the missing foxes?"

"That's right, Detective," I replied.

The detective nodded. "Good luck," he said. "Whoever cracks the case gets a huge reward. The zoo is offering ten thousand dollars to whoever brings those foxes back."

"Wow!" Cat said.

The detective glanced at his watch. "Well, kids," he said, "I better go. I'm about to make an arrest."

CHAPTER EIGHT

MORE SPYING

Detective Jones walked away.

My friends and I looked at each other.

Then we quickly hurried after Detective Jones.

"An arrest?" I said. "Already?"

"Who is he going to arrest?" Cat asked.

Sam shrugged as we ran along. "I guess we're going to find out," she said.

Detective Jones stopped at the fox exhibit. Shari and Ms. Marlow were still there.

"Where's Ed Mars?" the detective demanded. "I hear he's been hanging around here."

Shari and Ms. Marlow glanced at each other. "Ed Mars was out in front earlier," Shari replied. "He and his organization were protesting again."

"Protesting, huh?" the detective said. "Against what? Something about the foxes?"

"No, not the foxes," Ms. Marlow replied. "The Animal Protectors are protesting the gorillas' small living space."

Shari frowned. "It's true," she said. "The gorillas' space is too small. The AP likes to remind us."

"Hmm," the detective said. "And Mars hasn't been seen at the fox exhibit today?"

"Not that I know of," Shari replied.

Just then, I heard someone giggling nearby. I tugged Gum's shirt and turned toward the sound of laughter.

Anton was trying to sneak past us behind some bushes.

"Let's follow him," Gum said.

As quietly as we could, Gum and I headed after Anton. Sam and Cat were right behind us.

Then Gum stepped on an empty water bottle. It crinkled loudly, and Anton turned and saw us. He took off like a shot.

"Get him!" Cat shouted.

We chased Anton around the curvy paths of the zoo. He ran past the snack bar and the employee building.

We were getting closer. Then he made a sharp turn past the reptile house.

"That way," Sam said, pointing.

We turned the corner as fast as we could. We didn't see Anton anymore, but we nearly ran into Mr. Moreno, the animal hunter!

CHAPTER NINE

PET MOUSE

Mr. Moreno had his back to us, so he didn't see us.

"Look!" Sam whispered.

"It's the hunter!" Gum whispered. "He's not alone."

We instantly jumped behind a bush to watch the hunter and another man. The hunter was holding his paycheck. **"Ten thousand smackeroos,"** he said.

"When do I get my share?" the other man said. "As your assistant, I get twenty percent, don't forget."

"I know, Toro, I know," the hunter replied. "As soon as this check clears, you'll get your money."

"I better," the assistant said. He slipped his hand into his jacket pocket and then immediately pulled it back out.

"Ouch!" Toro shouted. "Stupid mouse! He bit me!"

He reached back into his pocket and pulled out a mouse.

Cat nearly squealed. Sam had to cover Cat's mouth so we wouldn't be caught.

"I love mice!" Cat whispered.

"Shh," Gum said.

"What are you doing with that mouse in your pocket?" Mr. Moreno asked Toro.

I used my zoom lens to snap a quick shot of the little mouse. It was an ordinary gray mouse. It seemed to be trying to escape.

Toro quickly slipped the mouse back into his pocket. "This mouse?" he said. "Why, this is my pet mouse, of course."

"Pet mouse?" Mr. Moreno asked. "I never heard of you having a pet mouse."

"Sure," Toro replied quickly. "His name is, um, Mr. Squeakers."

"What a cute name!" Cat whispered to me.

"Let's get to the bank and cash this check," Mr. Moreno said. "You can play with your mouse later."

"I'll catch up with you," Toro said. "I have some things to do."

"Fine," the hunter replied. "Meet me at the truck in fifteen minutes." The two men shook hands. Then they walked off in opposite directions.

"That assistant is really odd," Gum said. "He seems sneaky. And also, who keeps their pet mouse in their pocket? That's really weird, if you ask me."

"I agree," I said.

Cat shrugged. "I don't know," she said. "If I had a pet mouse, I'd keep her in my pocket."

Sam shook her head. "You're a piece of work, Cat," she said. "A real piece of work."

We stepped out from behind the bush. Suddenly, though, we were all flat on our backs. Anton had run right into us!

"Aha!" Sam said. "Gotcha!"

WHAT FOXES?

We were all in a pile on the ground. Anton stood up first and wiped the dirt from his pants.

"Okay, okay," he said. "You don't have to knock us down."

That's when I saw that Anton wasn't alone. He was with two of his **weaselly friends.**

"What are you two doing here?" I asked as I got up and made sure my camera wasn't cracked.

"I told them to meet me here," Anton said. "Hey, I don't mind going to the zoo, but I'd rather hang out with my friends than with you dorks."

"So you didn't steal the foxes?" Gum asked.

"The foxes?" Anton said. "What foxes?"

Sam rolled her eyes. "The Island Foxes!" she said. "You know, the reason we're at the zoo?"

"Oh right," Anton replied with a shrug. "Those foxes. What happened to them?"

"They were stolen, you banana," Cat replied. "Where have you been?"

"We were looking at the snakes," Anton said. "And now we're going to get some ice cream. So bug off."

After that, Anton and his sidekicks walked off, laughing.

"I guess he didn't steal the foxes," I said.

"Where does that leave us?" Gum asked.

Sam sighed and said, "No closer to finding the foxes, I guess."

SOLVED!

The four of us walked slowly back to Ms. Marlow's van. It was time to head back to school.

"I can't believe this," I said.

"I was so sure it was Anton this time," Gum said sadly.

"You always think it's Anton," Sam pointed out.

"That's true," Gum admitted.

"He was missing and everything," Cat said. "I thought it was Anton too."

As we walked, I clicked through the pictures I had taken on the trip. Then I stopped for a moment on the pictures of Mr. Moreno and his assistant, Toro.

Suddenly, I stopped in my tracks.

"Guys," I said. "I know who took the foxes."

"Is your suspect Ed Mars?" Sam asked.

I shook my head. "Nope," I said.

"It was Ms. Marlow!" Gum said. "That cage in the van was a clue. I bet the missing foxes are in it right now!"

We were already at the van. I ran over to the back door and pulled it open. The cage was still there, and it was empty.

Gum scratched his head. "Okay, I guess not!" he said.

I smiled. "I knew the cage would be empty," I said.

Ms. Marlow was saying goodbye to our guide, Shari, and to Detective Jones. "Thanks for showing us around, Shari," she said. "And Detective, I hope you find that crook."

"Ms. Marlow?" I said, walking over to them.

"Yes, Edward?" Ms. Marlow replied. "What is it? We need to get you kids back to school."

"First we need to find Mr. Moreno, the animal hunter," I said.

"Mr. Moreno?" Sam asked. "He stole the foxes?"

I shook my head. "Nope," I said. "But he can help us find the man who did."

Shari and Ms. Marlow looked at Detective Jones.

"These kids are great at solving mysteries," Detective Jones said. "We should listen to them. Do you know where we can find Mr. Moreno?"

"Mr. Moreno parks his truck in the employee lot," Shari said. "This way."

We all followed Shari. She led us around the back of the zoo. As we got to the parking lot, a bright orange SUV was pulling out.

"Mr. Moreno!" Shari yelled. "Mr. Moreno! Please wait!"

"Now what?" Mr. Moreno replied as he stopped the SUV. "Please don't tell me you want your money back."

"Of course not," Shari replied.

"Where is your assistant, Mr. Moreno?" I asked.

"Toro?" Mr. Moreno replied. "He's in the back of the truck. We're on our way to the bank now to cash my check."

My friends and I ran to the back of the SUV and pulled open the tailgate.

"Hey, what's going on?" Mr. Moreno said. He jumped out of the driver's seat.

The tailgate opened with a loud squeak. There, squatting in the back of the little truck, was Toro. Next to Toro was a crate with airholes in it.

"What do you want?" Toro asked. He was holding a little mouse.

"What are you doing with that mouse?" Cat asked angrily.

"My guess is he's about to drop it into that crate," I said.

Shari looked at me, then at the mouse. "Aha," she said. "That's not just a mouse. It's supper."

"Supper?" Mr. Moreno said. "Wait a second, Toro, you told me that was your pet mouse. You said his name was Mr. Squeakers."

Toro rolled his eyes.

"And what animal likes to eat mice for supper?" I asked.

"Island Foxes," Detective Jones said. He leaned forward and opened the crate.

Two small foxes were inside. They huddled together at the back of the crate.

Detective Jones grabbed Toro by the arm and pulled him out of the truck. "You're under arrest," the detective said.

"I don't get it, Toro," Mr. Moreno said. "Why did you steal the foxes you helped to catch in the first place?"

"Isn't it obvious?" Toro replied. "I did it for the money."

"But you got paid for catching the foxes to begin with," Cat pointed out.

"Not enough, though," I said. "Right?"

Toro sneered. "I do all the work on our hunts," he said. "And I get hardly any of our pay."

"But if you turned in the stolen foxes, you'd get the $10,000 reward," I added.

"It was the perfect plan," Toro said. "Until you kids ruined it for me."

Detective Jones put Toro into a nearby police car and closed the door.

"Well, Shari," the detective said, "you got your foxes back."

"Thanks to the science club," Shari replied.

"I'm going to take this crook downtown and book him for foxnapping," the detective said.

"Don't forget attempted mouse murder!" Cat added with a laugh.

Just then, Anton walked up. "There you guys are," he said. "I've been waiting at Ms. Marlow's van forever."

"Anton," Ms. Marlow said, "your friends caught the man who stole the foxes."

Anton looked at me, Sam, Cat, and Gum. "What foxes?" he asked. "And besides, these dorks are not my friends."

"What are you going to do with the reward money?" Shari asked me.

I looked at my friends. "I think we'll donate it to the zoo," I said. "To make the gorilla cage bigger."

Cat smiled. Then we headed back to Ms. Marlow's van.

The field trip was over. Another mystery was solved.

literary news

MYSTERIOUS WRITER REVEALED!

SAINT PAUL, MN

Steve Brezenoff lives in St. Paul, Minnesota, with his wife, Beth, their son, Sam, and their small, smelly dog, Harry. Besides writing books, he enjoys playing video games, riding his bicycle, and helping middle-school students work on their writing skills. Steve's ideas almost always come to him in his dreams, so he does his best writing in his pajamas.

arts & entertainment

CALIFORNIA ARTIST IS KEY TO SOLVING MYSTERY – POLICE SAY

Early on, C. B. Canga's parents discovered that a piece of paper and some crayons worked wonders in taming the restless dragon. There was no turning back. In 2002 he received his BFA in Illustration from the Academy of Arts University in San Francisco. He works at the Academy of Arts as a drawing instructor. He lives in California with his wife, Robyn, and his three kids.